PENNY DRAWS

A BEST FRIEND

PENNY DRAWS
A BEST FRIEND

SARA SHEPARD

G. P. PUTNAM'S SONS

G. P. PUTNAM'S SONS
An imprint of Penguin Random House LLC, New York

Produced by Alloy Entertainment
30 Hudson Yards, 22nd floor • New York, NY 10001

First published in the United States of America by G. P. Putnam's Sons,
an imprint of Penguin Random House LLC, 2023

Library of Congress Cataloging-in-Publication Data
Names: Shepard, Sara, 1977- author.
Title: Penny draws a best friend / Sara Shepard.
Description: New York: G. P. Putnam's Sons, 2023. | Series: Penny draws |
Summary: Fifth grader Penny, who doodles to cope with anxiety,
worries that her best friend is drifting away.
Identifiers: LCCN 2022051267 (print) | LCCN 2022051268 (ebook) | ISBN
9780593616772 (hardcover) | ISBN 9780593616789 (epub)
Subjects: CYAC: Friendship—Fiction. | Anxiety—Fiction. | Doodles—Fiction. |
Diaries—Fiction. | LCGFT: Diary fiction. | Novels.
Classification: LCC PZ7.S54324 Pb 2023 (print) | LCC PZ7.S54324 (ebook) |
DDC [Fic]—dc23
LC record available at https://lccn.loc.gov/2022051267
LC ebook record available at https://lccn.loc.gov/2022051268

Printed in the United States of America

ISBN 9780593616772
1st Printing
LSCC

Design by Marikka Tamura and Suki Boynton • Text set in Decour

Henry and Kristian, this book is for you!

PENNY DRAWS
A BEST FRIEND

DEAR COSMO

Mrs. Hines, the Feelings Teacher, says I could start this with Dear Diary, but that feels like something girls do. *I'm* a girl, but I mean *certain* girls in my class. The girls who dance like they're famous TikTokers.

I'm looking at you, Riley Miller.

Riley Miller has been in my class since we sang "Mommy Made Me Mash My M&M'S" scales in baby sing-along, not that she'd ever admit that.

Last year, Riley started Putty Club. You know that fidget putty teachers let you bring to school that comes in a little tin and has a funny name like "Creative Warrior" or "Thinking Power"? Well, Riley had everyone line up their jars of putty at recess, and she rated them according to best smell.

Except she didn't let just *anyone* into Putty Club. Only her friends.

So my best friend, Violet Vance, and I came up with a rival club: *Muddy* Club. It was all about mud around school. Who knew mud at the baseball diamond was so different from mud underneath the slide? Anyone could join, but Muddy Club never took off. I started to think about all that dirt under my fingernails. Which is probably why I go to Mrs. Hines, the Feelings Teacher.

I do like the idea of writing this to someone, though. I thought about writing to my mom, but I worried my mom might stumble across this book and think she was actually *supposed* to read it.

I thought about writing to Violet. The notes we pass in class are doodles—it's sort of our thing. I also thought about writing this to my little brother, Juice Box, but he can't read yet, and even if he *could* read, he'd only want to read about monster trucks.

Then I came up with an idea. I can write to Cosmo, my dog. He can't talk, and he *probably* can't read, and he sometimes eats the TV remote, which keeps me up at night.

But Cosmo is loyal and nice and would never make me feel weird about anything I write in here. Also, Cosmo and I share some of the same fears. Storms. Fireworks. Balloons. Clowns. Cosmo gets me.

So there. I'm writing to Cosmo.

Glad we've established that.

HOW TO DRAW A BEST FRIEND

Dear Cosmo,

Look at me, writing to my dog! How does it feel to be my pen pal? Is it better than getting your butt scratched? I'm guessing not, but you seemed interested enough when I read you my first entry yesterday.

Anyway, Cosmo, today was the first day of school. This year, I'm in fifth grade. We're at the top of the elementary heap.

There are three options for homeroom teachers you can get in fifth grade. Together, they're like Goldilocks's three bears. Mrs. Dunphy is Too Strict. Ms. Letts is Too Annoyed All the Time. And Mr. Glenn is Just Right because his classroom is filled with inflatable animals, a life-size Frankenstein, constantly blinking Christmas lights, and a rotating disco ball. Every day at 3:00 p.m., kids come out of Mr. Glenn's class looking like they've spent too much time at Dave & Buster's. Everyone loves him.

Our parents got our homeroom assignments two days ago. I wanted Mr. Glenn, but I got Mrs. Dunphy, the strict one. I had my mom call Violet's mom,

We're gonna have some FUN!

Mrs. Dunphy   Ms. Letts   Mr. Glenn

as neither Violet nor I have phones of our own. Violet was at her last day of camp, but Mrs. Vance told me that Violet got Mrs. Dunphy for homeroom, too. I was so relieved.

I've really missed Violet. She was away at camp all summer. It was this special gymnastics camp upstate, and during the weekends off, she stayed with cousins who live nearby. Usually, we spend our summers making an epic mural out of all the extra cardboard in our garages, or making newscast videos, complete with weather alerts, neighborhood news, and commercials. I tried to do both those things on my own this summer, but I only managed to finish half a painting of a beluga whale on a medium piece of cardboard. I emailed Violet my newscast videos, though, and the few times we talked on the phone, she told me they were great. I was pretty proud of my special report on neighborhood lemonade stands.

But I hadn't even gotten to see Violet before school started because her family just picked her up from camp yesterday, and then she needed to get all her school supplies and some new shoes.

So I was very excited to see her on the sidewalk outside of school. Except, things started off a little rocky.

I felt like I had a million important things to tell Violet. I asked her how camp was. Violet seemed really excited.

Riley, as in Riley Miller? Poor Violet. I can't believe she hadn't mentioned that before. That must have been torture.

Violet and I have been best friends since the first day of second grade when we both picked the same pumpkin to paint. We both liked this one pumpkin so much, we decided to paint it together.

Ever since then, art has been our thing. Every year, we join Art Club, which takes place after school. We do a joint project for the school Art Show. And it's a tradition that we draw a portrait of each other and bring it as a gift on the first day of school. I know it's silly, because we usually spend the whole summer together, but it's a great little bonus on the first day. Last year, the drawing Violet made for me totally got me through a very stressful seating chart. I don't know what I would have done without it.

I worked hard on my portrait of Violet over the summer. Instead of drawing a realistic version of her, I thought I'd draw what Violet was all about as a best friend. In fact, I started thinking she could be a prototype for a YouTube tutorial on "How to Draw a Best Friend." It could go like:

1. First, draw big happy eyes that crinkle when you tell a funny joke.
2. Then draw her ears—don't forget to add the earrings you made out of bakeable clay last year. (We almost set the house on fire because we got the oven settings wrong!)
3. Next, draw her curly hair. Make it her normal color, *not* the color we tried to dye it with Kool-Aid. (It was supposed to be light pink, but it came out the color of a traffic cone.)
4. Think about the things you CAN'T see, too: like what she's good at, how her brain works, and what's inside her heart!
5. Remember to add inside jokes!

I folded the drawing like a card. I wrote those instructions on the front. On the inside, my How to Draw a Best Friend drawing came out like this:

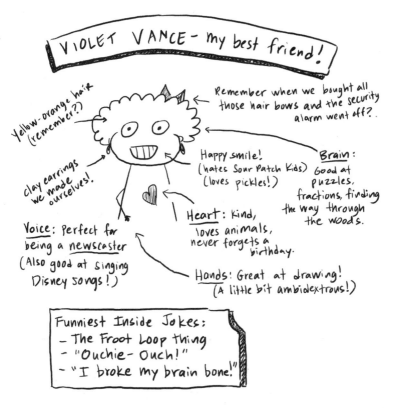

I was so excited to give it to Violet. I handed it to her on the sidewalk before we went inside.

She looked at my drawing for a long time.

And then she didn't say anything. I started to feel a little weird. Had I done something wrong? Had she forgotten about our tradition? But finally:

I have to say, the drawing of me looked suspiciously like a drawing Violet had done *last* school year before summer vacation. Like maybe she'd never taken it out of her backpack.

But it's okay. Violet probably didn't have time at camp to make a new drawing. And just because we've been separated all summer, it won't take us long to get our vibe back.

Seriously. This year is going to be great.

JUICE BOX

Dear Cosmo,

I should tell you about Juice Box, even though you probably already know him. Or . . . do you know that's his name? Maybe you only know him by smell. I read somewhere that when a dog smells stuff other dogs pee on, he's smelling secret messages in the other dogs' pee—messages only dogs understand. It's probably just things like *Hi there* and *I stole a piece of pizza* and *I like to sniff butts*, but what if the messages are much more important? I bet dogs are secretly really wise.

Anyway. Juice Box is my little brother. He's four. His real name is Noah, but we don't call him that anymore.

There's more to the story than that. See, Juice Box often gets this sickness called croup—which rhymes with *group, soup* . . . and, yes, *poop.* That joke's for you, Juice Box.

When you have croup, you suddenly can't breathe. It usually starts in the middle of the night, and there's not much parents can do except take you to the emergency room—especially if you panic, like Juice Box does. Most times, my parents both want to go, so I get dragged along, too.

At first, it was a real adventure to be awake at 3:00 a.m. But the emergency room got really boring, really fast.

Juice Box was always really distressed. Having trouble breathing looked scary. But the doctors and nurses never seemed concerned. Sometimes it took them a while to even come into the exam room. I never understood why they weren't trying everything to help him.

While we waited for the doctors, the only thing that ever calmed Juice Box down was when the nurses brought him juice. It took his mind off having trouble breathing. It was kind of magical. Juice Box got croup so often that it got to the point where as soon as Juice Box came through the ER doors, the nurses and doctors would be like:

The doctors started calling him Juice Box, too. And then everyone at the hospital did. Juice Box loved that he had a special name. So at preschool sign up earlier this summer, Juice Box made an important decision.

Anyway. This morning, we had to take Juice Box to preschool. That's not always easy. It especially wasn't easy this morning. It was the second day of school, and I wanted to get to the sidewalk early so I could talk to Violet before class. Yesterday, we'd all been so busy with first-day stuff that we barely talked. And after school, Violet said she couldn't come over.

But Juice Box was dragging his feet. Or, I should say, his wheels.

See, Juice Box loves monster trucks, and one of his favorite things is to pretend he's a famous monster truck driver. The name of his monster truck is The Juice.

Anyway, the longer Juice Box pretended he was driving The Juice, the later he was to preschool. And

since Mom was dropping me off second, that meant the later I was to *my school.*

When we pulled up to Juice Box's preschool, Juice Box started crying because monster truck drivers don't go to school. My mother hauled him out by his feet. Then Juice Box became what we call a "washrag."

I was really late. I definitely missed my chance to hang out with Violet on the sidewalk. In fact, the bell was probably ringing RIGHT NOW.

I pictured my class walking in and putting their stuff in their lockers. What was I missing? What if we were having a first-week-of-school test? What if Mrs. Dunphy was making an important decision that would determine the rest of the year—like where everyone was going to sit, or who we'd permanently be paired up with for projects? I wanted to be with Violet, but if I was late, I would be stuck with whoever was left. It wouldn't be someone nice, like Maria Mendes or Charlie Grove. It would be someone who didn't want to do any of the work. Or Liam Klauss, who kicks the back of people's desks. Or Sarah Philips, who was snobby and would do *all* the work and then my teacher would *know* and I'd get an F.

Or Rocco Roman. Oh no. What if I got Rocco Roman?

ROCCO ROMAN

Fists as big as honey-baked hams

Scratches from fights (probably)

Wears shorts EVEN IN WINTER!

By the time Juice Box calmed down and my mother got back to the car, I was shaking. She took one look at me and then made her Uh-Oh face. She told me it was going to be okay. But I didn't feel okay.

I don't remember the drive to my school. But I do remember it starting to rain, and my mom getting the striped umbrella to walk me through the front, saying that maybe instead of going into my classroom, I should take a little breather.

I remember my wet sneakers making a slapping sound on the waxy floor as I walked down the hall. I remember Violet catching my eye through the classroom window and then looking away.

And finally, I remember falling into the chair in Mrs. Hines's office.

THE FEELINGS TEACHER

Dear Cosmo,

The Feelings Teacher's real name is Mrs. Hines. She says that instead of teaching math or social studies, she teaches feelings. She has an office on the second floor of the building next to the Maker's Space, which is basically a crafting room where kids get to make sculptures with Popsicle sticks and cotton balls and way too much glue.

Here are some things I like about Mrs. Hines's room.

1. You get to learn feelings in a comfy chair instead of a desk. Which is great because

this year, I discovered my desk had a message written on the inside of it that I can't stop thinking about.

Who is Bug Man?
What does that mean?

2. There is a jar of candy on the coffee table. A candy jar violates the rule about no snacks at school, but Mrs. Hines says it's our little secret.

3. Mrs. Hines never laughs at anything I say, even if some of it sounds really silly. Like this morning, when I told her about my concerns, she said:

When someone has to make up a test, the teacher has them do it in the walk-in supply closet that's at the back of the classroom—it's a storage space for extra construction paper and glue and stuff. But Mrs. Hines clearly needed someone to explain that taking the test in these rooms is the worst possible thing because every single supply closet in every single classroom has the same mysterious fart smell.

I started talking to Mrs. Hines when I was in second grade. It's nice because I get to miss class and no one minds. A lot of the time, we don't even talk about worries. Sometimes we talk about dogs. Sometimes we talk about Art Club. Today, after Mrs. Hines assured me that I wasn't missing a test, I told her about how I was excited for this year. I was finally a fifth grader. And Violet and I always did fun things in the fall.

Apple picking   Leaf raking/jumping   Trick-or-treatin

Mrs. Hines asked if Violet was in my class, and how that was going.

After talking to Mrs. Hines, I felt a lot better—enough that I was able to go to class. But when I came out of Mrs. Hines's office, there was another kid in the waiting room.

I couldn't believe it. I've never *ever* seen another kid in the Feelings Teacher's office. This other kid was sitting in the chair, playing the peg game. You know the peg game? It's shaped like a triangle, and you have to jump the pegs until there's only one left?

I told him that was okay. I didn't know how many people had touched the peg game, and I didn't want to pick up any germs. Besides, I can never get down to just one peg.

Then the kid kept talking.

He seemed to want to talk even *more*, but sometimes I don't know what to do around people I don't know. So I mumbled something like "mrhthtff" and left.

But I didn't leave right away. I watched as Mrs. Hines opened the door to her office and greeted the kid. She had a big, friendly, welcoming smile, and called him by his name. It sounded like Christopher. Then Mrs. Hines caught my eye and gave me a wink. I felt sort of bad, like I was spying.

Still, though. I didn't realize anyone else needed the Feelings Teacher.

I thought it was only me.

ART CLUB

Dear Cosmo,

I've read that dogs' brains aren't very big, so in case you don't remember, you should try not to throw up inside the house anymore. This morning, you threw up right in the doorway of Mom and Dad's bedroom, and Dad stepped in it. The throw-up was made of tiny chewed-up plastic wheel from one of Juice Box's monster trucks. So by 7:00 a.m., two out of the four members of my house were in tears.

That was a rough start to my day, but I still had a good outlook. That's because today was the first day of Art Club. Art Club meets after school in this little classroom next to the library. I was glad I'd finally get to hang out with Violet. School has been so busy, we've hardly had a chance to talk.

Most of the same people from last year's Art Club showed up again. Like this kid Jesse, who's in fourth. All he did last year was take the *H* encyclopedia, open it to the entry on the human body, trace the page about the digestive organs, and color them vibrant colors with big arrows around them. I think he did that to gross out the girls.

Petra was back, too. She only draws Pokémon characters. She also speaks in this squeaky voice and maybe thinks she *is* a Pokémon.

I like Art Club for three reasons: First, I like to draw. Second, I like the teacher who runs it, Mr. Howdy. That's really his name, Mr. Howdy. Except he doesn't look like a cowboy; he looks like a yeti.

I wasn't sure about Mr. Howdy at first. I was afraid there was something *living in his beard*, like the rumors said. But he's very nice.

The third reason I like Art Club is obviously because Violet and I do it together. Violet also does gymnastics, and I tried lessons too for a while, but that didn't work out.

When I got to Art Club today, Violet was just hanging in the doorway.

I didn't understand. How is someone suddenly *not into drawing*? That's like not being into ice cream. Or waking up one day and deciding that everything on YouTube, all eleven bazillion videos, were boring.

For babies?!

Then Violet turned and walked down the hall. There was a girl waiting near the exit. It was . . . *Riley Miller.*

Riley and Violet started giggling. Then they looked right at me. *I* was the thing that was funny.

I didn't even know Violet *liked* Riley. One time, Violet said Riley's voice sounded like a pterodactyl's. Another time, Violet said Riley was so mean to a kid at lunch that the kid threw up macaroni and cheese through his nose. I'm not sure if that last part is true, but I bet Riley did do something really mean.

Who would want to be friends with that person? Did this happen at camp over the summer? Why hadn't Violet told me?

Mr. Howdy put his big yeti hand on my shoulder and said that Art Club was starting. I swallowed a lump in my throat. I guessed going into the library was better than standing and watching Violet walk away with Riley.

Jesse was in there, already working hard on a drawing of the small intestine. Petra hadn't changed, either: She'd created a creature called a Squintel that she said was a powered-up version of a Squee or something. No one in Art Club had changed. Except Violet. And maybe me.

Because suddenly, I sort of felt like I no longer had a best friend.

THE TARGET GAME

Dear Cosmo,

You didn't throw up this morning, yay! We all thank you. Especially Juice Box, who is still upset because of that chewed-up wheel.

Unfortunately, *I* felt like I had to throw up all night. I couldn't stop thinking about what had happened at Art Club. Violet telling me it was for babies. Violet walking away with Riley. I thought Violet would call me after school to explain . . . but she didn't. Not after school. Not in the evening. Not before bedtime.

Had she ditched me . . . for Riley? *Why?* What had I done? And also, did Violet really think

Riley was going to be careful about her tree nut allergy like I always am? And would Riley watch the gymnastics routines Violet was preparing for her meets—even if Violet performed them six times in a row?

And c'mon. Did Violet really think she and Riley would make better newscast videos than she and I did?

But then, were newscasts for babies, too?

Today was Saturday. And that means my mom, Juice Box, and I went to Target, as usual. At least *that* was the same.

When we got there, Juice Box wanted to play the Target Game. The Target Game is where Mom gives us a list of random stuff and we have to quickly find it. Usually, we do this together, but since I'm in fifth grade now, my mom asked if I'd like to look for items alone. I said okay. I needed to be more grown up, I figured. I kept thinking about what Violet said about Art Club. That it was *for babies*.

So my mom gave us the list.

I ran off through the store. The first thing I spotted was pink nail polish, so that worked for the something pink.

A cleaning product was easy to find, too. Paper towels were in the next row. They were a little awkward to carry.

It took me a little while to think of something with a cow on it, though. Farm toys? Juice Box went through a farm phase a while back. He was convinced all farm animals said moo. Horses said moo. Ducks said moo. The farmer said moo. The barn said moo.

And then I thought of something. Milk!

I went to the dairy section and found a gallon jug of milk with a cow on it. I was so excited. I found all the items! Maybe I'd won!

But then I realized. We hadn't planned a spot to meet when we finished.

I walked up and down the aisles, calling my mom's name, but she and Juice Box were nowhere.

My heart started to pound. The milk was getting really heavy. I hated that I was worrying—only *babies* cried when they got separated from their moms in Target. Just like only *babies* went to Art Club.

But what if something had *happened* to her? What if my mom had been kidnapped? What if Juice Box had a medical emergency and was in an ambulance? What if a giant display of Halloween costumes fell on them?

I felt tears on my cheeks. I couldn't breathe. These women kept passing, and they all looked like moms, but no one seemed to notice I was in distress. And then, down an aisle that sold vacuum cleaners, I saw Rocco Roman. Remember the kid I didn't want to get paired with for group projects? Yeah. Him.

Rocco Roman was looking at me. He was going to laugh, I just knew it.

I turned away from Rocco. But my mom still wasn't anywhere.

I hated the Target Game. I didn't know what to do. I started to melt into a puddle. This time, *I* was being the washrag. Next thing I knew, I was on the floor of Target, which was definitely covered in bacteria, curled into a ball. I tried to do the breathing exercise Mrs. Hines taught me, the one where you breathe in and hold it for a certain amount of time, but my brain felt like mud, and I couldn't think of any numbers.

And then I heard:

When I opened my eyes, my mom and Juice Box were standing there. They were holding a pink flamingo stuffie, a bottle of window cleaner, and the same jug of milk I had.

My mom put her hand gently on my back and said everything was okay. When I stood up, a lot of people were looking at me. Even Rocco Roman, who hadn't moved from his spot by the robot vacuums. *It isn't funny*, I wanted to tell him. But still, I felt like such a baby.

At least Violet hadn't seen.

THAT OTHER KID

Dear Cosmo,

You got a rabies shot this morning. I know it probably wasn't fun, but it's better than you getting bitten in the wild and spreading rabies to us. Not only would we not be able to keep you, I've heard a rumor that we'd also all have to get shots in our stomachs. IN OUR STOMACHS.

So thanks for taking one for the team.

Today was Monday. On Mondays, I meet with Mrs. Hines. I had a lot to talk about. Lying on the floor at Target. Rocco Roman. And I *really* wanted to talk to her about Violet. I was still afraid to ask Violet what was going on. And I really didn't understand why she suddenly liked Riley Miller. What magical thing happened at camp that made Violet want to be Riley's friend?

I tried to write Violet a letter asking her this, but it didn't go well.

Anyway. This morning, I made sure to get to school early so I could hang out on the sidewalk. Violet was there . . . *with Riley again!*

I brought up the soccer tournament because that's the reason Violet gave for not being able to hang out this weekend. The tournament was out of town, she said, and her whole family had to go. But by the looks on Riley's and Violet's faces, I started to think maybe there *wasn't* a soccer tournament.

It made me get that throw-up feeling again.

I was in a fog that morning during social studies and language arts, so much so that Mrs. Dunphy seemed to notice. She told me I could go to Mrs. Hines's office a little bit early. When I got there, Mrs. Hines's door was closed. I was surprised to see that other kid sitting in her waiting room again. Like last time, he was playing the peg game. He definitely remembered me.

My life sometimes felt like a perilous journey, so that sort of worked. I wasn't sure I wanted a nickname after a roller coaster, though. Or pajamas.

DEAR stands for Drop Everything And Read. It's basically silent reading, but I think it's really so teachers can have a little break from us. Last year during DEAR Time, I had to use the bathroom, so I stepped into the hall to find a teacher so she could give me a pass. But my teacher wasn't in the hall, which made me worry something had happened to her. Maybe something had happened to *all* the teachers in the building—like an alien ship came down and stole away all the teachers, leaving all the students alone!

I worked myself up into believing that was true. But then I heard whispering coming from a little room across the hall.

The teachers were talking about their students! *That's* what they did during DEAR Time?

Anyway, I found out the kid in Mrs. Hines's office is named Kristian, not Christopher. He's in Ms. Letts's fifth-grade class. I've seen Kristian around school, but we've never been in the same class.

I was curious. Like I said before, I didn't know anyone else visited Mrs. Hines. But there he was, just chilling at the table like it was his living room.

I had to agree with him there. Mrs. Hines *is* really nice.

I don't like roller coasters. You're strapped into a little car, sometimes with only a seat belt, going super fast. How is that fun?

But I have to say, Kristian looked pretty happy. He didn't even have any broken bones.

Then Mrs. Hines's door opened. And I couldn't believe it.

One other kid in Mrs. Hines's office was something. But *two*? My mind was blown.

Especially because the second kid was Maria Mendes. Maria! What does *she* need a Feelings Teacher for?

MARIA

Dear Cosmo,

Even *you* know Maria Mendes. Remember that one time Mom brought you to school pick-up? Sometimes people bring their dogs, and all the dogs patiently wait at the top of the stairs because no dogs are allowed on school property.

Except you didn't wait patiently. You saw a squirrel on the lawn and wiggled out of your collar and went running

toward the flagpole.

Cosmo! Come back RIGHT NOW! You'll get me kicked off the PTA!

Then the bell rang, and everyone came out. The reason dogs aren't allowed on school property is probably so they don't poop on the school lawn. It's probably also because some kids are afraid of dogs. And, Cosmo, when you're after a squirrel, you look sort of scary.

Kids ran screaming. Parents glared at my mom, who was desperately trying to get you off the lawn, but you didn't listen. Then Maria appeared.

I guess Maria never got the message that you shouldn't pet strange dogs because they might bite off your hand, but it was all good. Once everyone realized you were nice, then *other* kids gathered around you, and you went from being the Terror Dog That Ate Small Children to the Best Doggie in the Schoolyard. Maria is *magical*.

Here are other reasons Maria is great.

1. She always has amazing Halloween costumes.

MR. PEANUT   MAC AND CHEESE   BATMOBILE

2. This one time in gym, Maria's class was playing kickball. Every time Rocco Roman was up, I swear he tried to kick the ball

at people's heads. Like Carly Thomas's, when Carly was playing outfield.

But *then* this happened.

3. Everyone likes Maria, but it's not because she leaves people out, like Riley. She includes everyone. She also didn't join Putty Club even though Riley really, *really* wanted her. Maria said it was because she didn't like that putty was sticky, but I also like to think it's because she didn't think Riley was very nice.

So I have no idea why Maria visited with Mrs. Hines, the Feelings Teacher. She seems so perfect.

Then I realized something as she was leaving. Maria and Violet walk the same route to school. It's often a clump of kids walking together, and I know Maria and Violet sometimes talk. Maybe Violet had said something to Maria about her weekend, like if she'd hung out with Riley instead of going to a soccer tournament. Or why she'd ditched me.

I tried to ask Maria in a way that didn't make me sound too weird.

Just a week ago, I would have absolutely been able to answer that question. Yes. Yes, of course, Violet was my best friend.

But today? Today, everything was different.

THE AMAZING THING

Dear Cosmo,

Something amazing happened today after school. I can hardly believe it. It might not be that interesting to you because you're a dog, though. What *is* amazing to a dog? Finding an open jar of peanut butter on the floor? Rolling around in the perfect patch of mud? Getting to smell a whole bunch of other dogs' butts?

I'll start at the beginning.

When I got home from school, my mom grabbed me before I went into the kitchen.

Have a snack quickly. We're going to the mall.

Do we HAVE to?

I wasn't looking forward to it. Usually, when we go to the mall, it's for something boring (like my mom picking up a glasses prescription), something mortifying (buying me new underwear), or something scary (visiting the Easter Bunny).

Is anyone else really creeped out by the mall Easter Bunny? Why does he wear a vest but no pants?

Needless to say, I didn't have high hopes. We left Juice Box at home with my dad, which made me think it was going to be one of those trips for new underwear.

But when we got there, we walked right past

the underwear department. In fact, we walked out of the department store altogether. I was confused. What else could we be here for?

My mom seemed on a mission. She went right up the escalator to the second level. Past the pretzel stand. Past the stand that sells Pop It! fidget toys. Past the glasses place. And right toward . . .

I was pretty sure this was a joke. Except I'd checked the calendar, and it wasn't Opposite Day. See, everyone in my grade *wants* a cell phone, but every parent says we're too young to have one. And the thing is, I don't even want a cell phone so I can play Roblox or look up bad words. I needed a phone for other reasons. Actually, Mrs. Hines and I had talked about it.

Huh. Is it possible Mrs. Hines told my mom about this?

We walked into the cell phone store. We looked at shelves of phones and tried a few. I picked one that unfolded into the size of a tablet and had six camera lenses and a built-in wind machine. After looking at the price tag, my mother steered me toward the "starter phone" section.

I was sad not to have a built-in wind machine, but it was pretty amazing to have a phone of my own. With my own phone number! Once the guy at the store set it all up, I really wanted to text someone. Violet, maybe? But . . . she didn't have a phone. And anyway, I'm not sure she'd want to get a text from me.

In the end, I couldn't think of anyone my age to text, so I ended up texting my mom.

I texted my dad, too. He likes monkeys, so I sent him a bunch of monkey emojis.

Then, when I walked out of the store, I noticed two girls standing by the fountain. One of them was Riley Miller. The other was *Violet!* Since when was she allowed to go to the mall by herself?

Unfortunately, my mom spotted her, too.

Violet and Riley saw me. I saw them look right at my cell phone, too, which I was still holding. Their mouths dropped open. They nudged each other.

So I did the only thing I could think of: I lifted the phone to my ear and started talking just to make sure they understood *this* was *my* phone, not my mom's. Never mind that I wasn't actually talking to anyone. And never mind that my mom was looking at me a little worriedly.

It was the best fake conversation I'd ever had.

I glanced back at them as we went down the escalator. Violet was still watching me. And maybe I was seeing things, Cosmo, but I actually think she looked like she missed me.

And even though I don't want to miss Violet . . . I do.

THE GROUP

Dear Cosmo,

Sometimes I really wish I were a dog. I'd get to lie around all day in a square of sun. Someone would feed me chicken-flavored treats. I wouldn't have to listen to Riley and Violet whispering in class and wonder if they were whispering about *me*. I also wouldn't have to listen to Oliver Bracca, who sits in front of me and hums all day long.

If he isn't humming "The Star-Spangled Banner," then it's "My Country 'Tis of Thee" or "America the Beautiful." Oliver is very patriotic.

If I were a dog, I also wouldn't have to deal with the Math Relay Race, which Mrs. Dunphy started on the very first day of school. We're split into random pairs to see which pair can complete a relay of math facts the fastest. I bet you don't even *know* math facts, Cosmo. Quick: What's two times four? Or forty-two divided by six? Even if you do know those things, no one is ever going to ask you to figure them out *quickly*.

For today's Math Relay Race, I was paired with this kid Michael McMinnamin. Michael is enrolled in every sport and is competitive about everything, even math games.

Would I have liked to be paired with some-one else? Definitely. Michael took the fact that we came in third place REALLY HARD. That's another thing you're lucky you don't have to deal with as a dog, Cosmo: your teacher splitting you into random groups. Teachers say random groups help us learn to work with different types of peo-ple, but sometimes I lie awake at night thinking of who I might be paired with the next day.

After Math Relay Race was over, it was time for science. Mrs. Dunphy made an announce-ment that the Science Fair is coming up in a few weeks. Normally, that's a good thing. My last three Science Fair projects were deep dives into stuff I was concerned about anyway.

But this year, Mrs. Dunphy said she wanted us to work in teams of three, and the project would be a big part of our science grade for the first marking period. To make things fair, she said she would group us herself. Randomly.

Why do teachers always feel the need to *make things fair*? Why? And we already had one random group today: Math Relay Race. I wasn't sure if I could handle one more!

Mrs. Dunphy got the magician's hat she uses to pick the names for the groups. All our names were written on little pieces of paper, and she pulled names out one by one and started writing them on the board. She said that our groups were free to choose our own Science Fair topic, but we should run it by her first so that no two groups did the same project.

Everyone was talking excitedly, but I felt like there were bugs crawling under my skin. I didn't want to work in a group. I wanted to work by myself. Except I *couldn't* work by myself because then I'd get an F in science.

Oliver's humming was *not helping*. Then I saw Mrs. Dunphy write my name at the top of a new group. My heart started to pound. I

waited to see whose names she'd pull out next, bargaining with the universe. I could deal with being paired with Oliver Bracca or even Michael McMinnamin. But please not Cobie Wilder. Cobie's Science Fair projects always involve explosions. No thank you.

Then Mrs. Dunphy called out two more names.

I couldn't believe it. *What were the chances?*

I heard Riley and Violet whispering again. I felt them looking at me. My palms prickled. I felt hot, and then cold, and then hot again. Mrs. Dunphy said something else, but her voice sounded like an air horn. I couldn't deal with being in a group with Riley *and* with Violet, who wasn't speaking to me anymore. I just *couldn't*.

And then everything went black.

I'm pretty sure I just died.

THE DARKNESS

Dear Cosmo,

I thought there would be dogs in the afterlife. And clouds. And sunbeams, maybe? But in my afterlife, there was only darkness. The afterlife smelled bad, too. Like egg burps. And smelly sneakers. And the Spaghetti Special that the cafeteria makes on Wednesdays.

I felt embarrassed, too. Did I seriously just *die* because I'd been paired with Riley and Violet? My heart really stopped because of *that*?

Then I heard some humming that sounded like Oliver Bracca. What was *Oliver* doing in my afterlife? Then I heard another voice. I think it was Cobie Wilder, the kid who likes explosions. And . . . Mrs. Dunphy?

Okay, so maybe I wasn't dead. But math facts? Like *that* was going to go over well in a power outage or whatever this was?

Outside, branches scraped against the windows. I heard a thud and wondered if it was the flagpole falling over. If there was someone under it, they'd definitely be crushed. I wondered if we should be getting under our desks. Mrs. Dunphy had also hung clay models of airplanes we'd just made because we're learning about the Wright brothers. I did *not* want a ceramic biplane knocking me unconscious.

Then I remembered: my cell phone. Technically, I was supposed to put it in my cubby this morning, but I'd forgotten. It was still in my pocket.

I pulled it out and called my mom.

I stood up and whispered to Mrs. Dunphy that I was leaving. I think she heard me, but it was hard to tell over everyone chanting multiplication tables.

In the hallway, I used the phone light to get to Mrs. Hines's room. Thankfully, her door wasn't locked. There wasn't any power here, either. Still, when I walked into the waiting room, I could tell someone else was in there.

I told them who I was, too. Huh. Maria, Kristian, and I all had the same idea.

Then I said I was here because I was afraid a model airplane was going to fall on my head. Maria and Kristian had the same concerns, except they were worried about the whales their class had made falling on *their* heads. I've seen those whales. Maria and Kristian's class built ginormous models for the "Largest Mammals" chapter in science. Kids kept bumping their heads on them.

And then I was like:

I have no idea why a kid our age would read up on the school's building codes, but I was glad Kristian had. It made me feel a lot better.

Then Maria said she and Kristian were passing the time by talking about the best birthday gifts they'd ever gotten. Kristian said his was getting a Fast Pass to ride the Head Chopper over and over again. Maria said hers was a handmade bracelet from her favorite aunt. Then they asked me what mine was.

The answer is obvious: It was getting *you*, Cosmo.

The day I turned seven, my parents said happy birthday, but then they said they had to go shopping. Juice Box and I had to stay with a babysitter—and not even the *nice* babysitter, but the boring teenager who never left the couch.

I was so mad. It was my birthday! I didn't want to spend it with a babysitter!

An hour later, my mother came back into the house, saying that something had happened to the car and I needed to come see. I thought they'd gotten into a car accident and there was a big dent. Or maybe the car was on fire, and then we wouldn't have a car to get around anymore, and we'd have to walk everywhere, even in the snow.

But instead, there was something waiting for me in the back seat.

I smiled as I told this story. Kristian and Maria thought it was a great gift. They both said they loved dogs.

It was nice talking to them. It made me forget about the power outage or being paired with Riley and Violet.

The lights snapped on again, and we looked at each other and smiled. Outside, it was still cloudy, but the storm clouds had passed.

Then I realized something. We were sitting in Mrs. Hines's waiting room, but where was Mrs. Hines? This seemed to occur to Kristian and Maria, too, because we all looked at her closed door at the same time.

And then . . . the door opened. And once again, there was *another kid* with the Feelings Teacher.

Rocco *Roman*?

ROCCO ROMAN

Dear Cosmo,

Does anything blow a dog's mind? One time, you had peanut butter stuck to the end of your nose, but you couldn't figure out how to lick the peanut butter off—your tongue didn't quite reach. You licked and licked for a long time. You really did seem like your head was going to explode.

All of us stared when Rocco Roman came out of Mrs. Hines's office. I wouldn't have been more surprised if a werewolf had walked out.

Here are some things to know about Rocco Roman.

1. He's eighth-grader big. The librarian has him get books on the high shelves

for smaller kids. He always seems really annoyed with having to do that.

2. Because he's so big, rumor has it that Rocco has driven a car and gone to PG-13-rated movies without a parent's supervision.

3. The most legendary rumor about Rocco—the thing no one forgets—is that one day in kindergarten, this kid David was sitting next to Rocco and decided to steal some of Rocco's Play-Doh. Rocco got so angry that he grabbed David's hands and squeezed them like they were stress balls. David screamed, and his hands turned purple, and he even had to go home for the rest of the day.

But here was Rocco in Mrs. Hines's office. Even weirder, Mrs. Hines was being nice to Rocco, like they were friends. She looked at us, surprised that we were all gathered in her waiting room.

Then the phone in Mrs. Hines's office started to ring, so she had to answer it, LEAVING US ALONE WITH ROCCO. It led to a very uncomfortable staring contest.

I can't believe Kristian dared to speak to Rocco. Rocco was probably going to use the peg game as a weapon on him. Or he was going to lock us all in the custodian's closet next door, which I know for a fact contains flammable chemicals.

But instead, Rocco said something surprising.

I guess Rocco didn't really care if we were impressed, because he got out of there fast. But I have to say, that's a cool gift. If you aren't afraid of helicopter rides, that is.

Not as good a gift as you, Cosmo, but pretty close.

JUGGLING KNIVES

Dear Cosmo,

You bark a lot. Sometimes Mom gets really mad at you, especially if you bark at things that aren't there.

Barking doesn't solve everything. It doesn't make that leaf go away, or that squirrel move any faster, or that weird stone pineapple our neighbor put by her mailbox disappear.

Turns out, a cell phone doesn't solve everything, either.

My head was spinning on the way home from school. I couldn't believe Rocco Roman talked to Mrs. Hines: Now, whenever I went in there, I'd have to worry about seeing him.

I also couldn't believe our school had lost power for thirty-four minutes. Was this going to be an ongoing trend? Were we going to lose power *regularly*?

And I *really* couldn't believe I was in the Science Fair group with Riley and Violet. I tried to make a list of all the things that could go wrong during the project or ways I might embarrass myself. What if Violet called me a baby in front of Riley? *What if I got so nervous, I peed my pants?* That happened once, in line for a haunted house. When I heard a werewolf growl inside, the pee just let loose.

Come to think of it, I'd *told* Violet that. I thought I could trust her. But what if she told

Riley . . . and what if Riley told THE WHOLE SCHOOL?

These were way too many worries for me to handle. I felt like that lady we saw on the beach boardwalk during our summer vacation, the one who was juggling torches. After a while, she switched it up and started juggling KNIVES.

When I got home from school, I noticed that Juice Box was sitting all alone in front of the TV, watching last year's Monster Jam. *That* was odd. My parents never let Juice Box watch TV by himself because he always sits too close to the TV, and my mom thinks it's going to destroy his brain.

I looked around for my parents. Then I heard whispering from the laundry room.

They were standing in the room acting like nothing was wrong, which was a dead giveaway that *something was very wrong.*

That wasn't so suspicious. *None* of us want to go to Monster Jam, which was coming up this weekend. We went last year, too, and it smells like exhaust, it's really loud, and the trucks catch fire, which seems like a major hazard. But we all do it for Juice Box.

A *prior commitment*? My mom is a mom. She doesn't *have* prior commitments. And I'd rather juggle knives than ask Violet to Monster Jam. Even when we *were* still friends, I wouldn't have done that to her. I'm pretty sure my mom knows something's up with Violet, though. This morning, she came into my room with a bunch of questions.

But anyway. After my parents were being weird, they left the room like none of this was a big deal.

Way too many possibilities whirled through my mind. *Why were they really whispering?* Was someone sick? Was someone *dead*? Were the walls in our house full of bugs? Were we moving somewhere awful? Were they getting *divorced*?

I glanced at Juice Box. He didn't seem to think anything was up, but then, he's four. The most important thing to Juice Box besides monster trucks is the color of his boogers.

But I felt awful. Because you know what's even worse than knowing something terrible is about to happen?

Being *lied to* about it.

INTESTINES

Dear Cosmo,

Sorry I was a little scattered this morning. It's just that when you have SO MANY THINGS ON YOUR MIND, it's perfectly normal to forget to do your chores.

Today was the first day that we split up into the groups to work on the Science Fair project. And I was ready.

Sort of.

Actually, I wasn't ready at all. I was a ball of nerves. But I brought my mother's lavender eye mask to school. You know the one Mom sometimes puts over her face when she lies down in the middle of the day? One time, she lay with the lavender mask on her eyes for a whole hour. I bet you remember that, Cosmo. It was when Juice Box painted you purple.

Anyway, I slipped out of my desk right before science, snuck to the supply closet in the back of the classroom, and put the lavender mask over my eyes. The room smelled like farts, as usual, but I hoped the lavender smell from the mask would overpower it.

I closed my eyes and sat in the darkness, breathing in the calming lavender. I was starting to feel better. That didn't last long, though, because Oliver Bracca chose that exact moment to show up, looking for some extra pencils or something.

He said it like I was really weird, but he's one to talk! This morning, Oliver hummed all of the different instrument parts to "The Stars and Stripes Forever."

I had no choice but to go back to my desk. Everyone was already sitting with their part-ners, so I took the walk of doom over to Riley and Violet. They sat next to Cinnamon the gerbil's cage. Don't let the cute name fool you. Cinnamon has DEVIL EYES.

I sat down and tried to ignore the fact that Cinnamon was trying to steal my soul. I waited for Riley and Violet to say something mean to me, but they barely noticed I was there.

But maybe that was better than the alternative. Maybe they'd just talk to each other the whole time. We'd get nothing done, and we'd have no science project, and I'd have to repeat fifth grade, which would probably set me back for life, but at least I wouldn't be made fun of.

Then Mrs. Dunphy had to come by and ruin it.

Thanks for asking *us*, Riley.

I couldn't believe Mrs. Dunphy put me on the spot like that. My mind was blank. In the moment, I couldn't even come up with that baking-soda-and-vinegar volcano project you see at *every* Science Fair.

Time was ticking. Violet and Riley were staring at me. I NEEDED TO SAY SOMETHING. Then I noticed someone walking down the hall.

It was Jesse, the kid in Art Club who always drew the digestive system. And I don't know why, but the word just popped out of my mouth.

Mrs. Dunphy thought it was a wonderful idea. She said they could probably get us a frog from the middle school. Students would love to see how a frog's organs are similar to a human's.

But I didn't want to dissect a frog! And Riley *definitely* didn't want to dissect a frog, and Violet was looking at me like I'd committed a MAJOR CRIME.

But Mrs. Dunphy seemed so pleased. She was already writing it down on her clipboard as our official Science Fair project.

I turned to Violet and Riley. Maybe if I smiled in a friendly way, they'd let this slide?

Way to go, Penny. Just so you know, you're touching ALL the guts.

Guess not.

FOLD UP

Dear Cosmo,

Do dogs need Feelings Teachers? You have a lot of feelings—sometimes you're Happy Dog, other times you're Ashamed Dog. Then there's Hungry Dog and Wild Squirrel Dog. Doesn't it get tiring feeling all those things?

It was a good thing I was able to see Mrs. Hines after the Great Intestines Disaster, as I've started to call it. When I got to her office, her waiting room was empty. I walked right in and fell into her chair. When she asked me what the matter was, I couldn't speak for a good thirty seconds.

Then it all came out in a jumble.

Mrs. Hines had me slow down and take one issue at a time. She wanted to know about Violet. I'd told her Violet quit Art Club, and that, all of a sudden, we weren't friends anymore.

When I said *I guess*, I was trying to be cool. *I guess* really meant *absolutely*, and *this is maybe the worst thing that's happened to me.*

Mrs. Hines asked about things I missed about Violet. I told her I missed the acorn fights we had with her neighbors. I missed the scavenger hunts we made after school. I missed how, during lunch, we used to play a game called Fold Up, where one person draws a head, then folds the paper down and passes it, then the next person draws a

body, then folds *their* part up and passes it back, and the other person draws legs and feet.

Thinking about our Fold Up creations made me want to cry. I bet Violet didn't even bring her art stuff to lunch anymore. She's been sitting with Riley. *At their own table.*

And I was still so upset about the best friend portrait thing.

I worked so hard on this drawing for her. It was perfect. And she gave me a SCRIBBLE!

From last year!

Why don't you ask her what's going on?

That's a TERRIBLE idea!

Why?

Because...

What if Violet's reason for no longer liking me was something I already knew? What if it was something I *didn't* already know? I couldn't decide which was worse.

And here's the thing: I thought Violet liked everything about me, even the things most people *didn't* like. Isn't that the way a best friend is sup-posed to be? They're supposed to accept all your quirks, like how I peel the cheese off the pizza and *then* eat the dough and *then* eat the crust. I certainly accepted everything about her. Like that she gets cranky when she's tired. And that she never wants to ride bikes because secretly, she never learned how.

We'd spent so much time together. I thought we'd be best friends forever.

I guess I was wrong.

A ROMANCE FOR ALL AGES

Dear Cosmo,

Do you ever worry that, when we leave, we aren't going to come back? My mom always tells me that dogs have no concept of how much time has passed—it can be five hours, but to a dog, it feels like five minutes. I'm not sure about that, though. You seem to know exactly when it's dinnertime. And you do this magical thing where you sit at the window five minutes before my dad pulls onto our street, no matter what time it is.

Our school is a walking district, meaning there are no buses. But we live across a busy road with lots of traffic, so Mom usually drives me and picks me up. I'm glad I don't have to ride a bus, by the way. When I was on a kindergarten field trip, our bus got a flat tire, and the bus driver, this old lady named Beatrice, had no idea what to do.

I thought we were going to be stuck on the side of the road forever.

Anyway, today after school, I was waiting for my mom up at the Drop-Off Zone. The Drop-Off Zone is policed by Mrs. Wink. Mrs. Wink takes her job very seriously.

One time, I saw Mrs. Wink in the window of a beauty salon with big curlers in her hair. She looked like an alien. An alien with lipstick on. It was very bizarre.

I was waiting in the Drop-Off Zone, watching Mrs. Wink yell at everyone. My mom was late, but I figured she was in the back of the line of cars. Then Maria came up next to me. Maria normally walked home with Violet and some others, so I was surprised she wasn't gone already.

Maria explained that she was in the school-wide Spelling Bee and needed to practice. The Spelling Bee is serious business. The person who wins gets to wear a bee-shaped hat for a week, *and* they get free ice cream for lunch. So I gave Maria some words.

I told Maria she was really good and would probably win. Maria said she hoped so—her sister had won the Bee when *she* was Maria's age. She also said I could come watch if I wanted. The Spelling Bee was in a few weeks, the day before the Science Fair.

Maria must have seen my smile fade, and then she said that I didn't *have* to come watch the Spelling Bee if I didn't want to. But that's not what changed my mood. I'd started thinking about the Science Fair again.

I almost told Maria about Violet, Riley, and the frog, but Maria is so cool. Science Fairs probably never bother her no matter who she gets paired with. I bet she never had a best friend just drop her for no good reason.

Then I checked my watch. My mom was *really late*. Was there a pileup somewhere on the interstate? Then I pulled out my phone. My mom had sent me a text saying she was on her way. She didn't say *why* she was late, though. My mind started to spiral. Maybe it had something to do with my parents whispering the other day. Could I ask Maria about *that*?

I decided to give it a shot.

I was pretty sure my parents weren't whispering about a neighbor. I'd narrowed down their secret to two possibilities: Someone was sick, or they were getting a divorce. Could that be it? Ugh. Two Christmases would stress me out.

Finally, my mom pulled up, nearly running

over Mrs. Wink. After Mrs. Wink yelled at her and blew her whistle, I opened the door. I spotted something on my mom's shirt as I got in.

My mom shifted her weight so I couldn't see the badge anymore. I'd only spotted her name, the date, and the time, but there was some other writing that was too small to read. It definitely seemed like she didn't want me to know what it was.

Suddenly, I had a feeling what she was up to.

Okay, my mom caught me. For the record, I only picked up that book at Rite Aid because my mom was taking so long with the pharmacist. And, fine, it *was* about a love affair between a woman and a man in prison—but it still was possible that's what my mom was doing!

And, yes, I should have realized that it was beyond my reading level when I saw the shirtless man on the cover.

In my defense, I thought the cover said "A Romance for *All* Ages"—meaning it would be okay if I read it.

My mom laughed at my accusation and said that no,

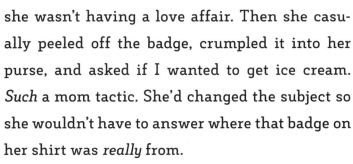

she wasn't having a love affair. Then she casually peeled off the badge, crumpled it into her purse, and asked if I wanted to get ice cream. *Such* a mom tactic. She'd changed the subject so she wouldn't have to answer where that badge on her shirt was *really* from.

But I was onto her. And I was going to figure it out.

OPERATION SMARTY PANTS

Dear Cosmo,

Today was Monster Jam day. We had to take Dad's car to get there because Mom was using her own car to do the SECRET THING SHE DIDN'T WANT TO TELL ANYONE ABOUT.

My dad's car is okay, except the stereo doesn't work. It's stuck on CD mode, and my dad can't figure out how to get a CD out of the player. If we want music, we have to listen to the same CD over and over again.

All the songs are about tractors. They're Juice Box's favorites.

At the stadium, we waited in line to get in. Of course, Juice Box was in full monster-truck-driver mode. Everyone else in line was, too. These were definitely Juice Box's people.

Once inside, Juice Box went straight to the merch table and selected twelve new monster trucks he just had to have for his collection. Dad negotiated Juice Box down to two.

When we took our seats, my dad promptly fell asleep. He can fall asleep *anywhere*.

I needed to put my plan into action. See, I knew my mother was lying about where she was today, and I was going to figure out what was going on. I called the plan OPERATION SMARTY PANTS. Why? Well, this morning, my mother was wearing new pants I'd never seen before. They were sort of . . . stretchy. I felt like it was an important clue.

My phone isn't the fanciest, but I'd been playing on it yesterday, and I noticed that there was an app called Track My Friends. It was totally going to come in handy. I could use it to always know where my mom was in case I ever got separated from her in Target again.

But I realized it had an even better use. I could track where she was *now*. I turned my phone on and clicked on the app. A window came up.

I was surprised my mom hadn't clicked the button on *her* phone to turn off her GPS tracking. If she was going somewhere so secretive, wouldn't that be a good idea? Then I realized she probably didn't even know her phone *had* GPS tracking. My mom is terrible with technology. She doesn't even know how to use the remote. Even Juice Box has it figured out.

I clicked a little button saying that I wanted the app to figure out my mom's location. My heart pounded as a little wheel spun and a message came up reading TRACKING IN PROGRESS.

To distract myself, I watched the trucks with Juice Box. It *was* kind of cool watching them do the backflips and wheelies. I didn't even mind when one of the trucks crashed and another caught fire and they had to bring out the extinguishers.

Juice Box said he thought the truck that looked like a zombie would win. I figured the one that didn't catch fire would win. Turned out, neither of us was right. The truck that won was called Monster Mutt. It looked like a Dalmatian. And it *did* catch fire, but apparently, that doesn't seem to matter in the world of monster trucks.

Then my phone pinged. LOCATION TRACKED. I was so nervous to read the results. My hands were shaking.

An office building?

That could mean anything!

RILEY'S HOUSE

Dear Cosmo,

Well, today was the day. The day I was supposed to work on the Science Fair project with Violet and Riley. I wasn't looking forward to it. Yesterday, I planned out who I'd pass my belongings to in case I didn't make it. I said you could have my stuffed animals, since you think they're dog toys anyway. But please don't tear my stuffed porcupine apart. I've had him since I was little. Babyish, I know, but I'd miss him.

We'd agreed to meet at Riley's to do our project. For most fifth-grade girls, it's a total win to have an invite to Riley Miller's house. So I figured the place had to be amazing. As in a mansion with three swimming pools, six kitchens, a pet potbellied pig, and a butler. I pictured parties happening nonstop, and a twisty slide instead of stairs, and a bathtub full of Skittles.

So when my dad pulled up to a curb and said we were here, I was confused.

That house looks like my house.

My dad said goodbye. I gave him a suspicious look. I hadn't gotten any closer to figuring out Operation Smarty Pants, otherwise known as why my mom skipped the monster truck show to hang out in an office building—but I bet he knew. What's in an *office building*? Copy machines? *Desks?* The only time *I'd* been dragged to an office building was for Juice Box's speech therapy last year. Oh, there was also the time we visited my mom's friend who teaches private meditation courses. Mom even made me try meditating, saying it would help calm me down. But it wasn't particularly helpful.

I stepped onto the curb in front of Riley's house. Then I noticed these amazing chalk drawings all along the driveway of the house next door. The drawings took up the whole driveway—whoever had done it must have been working on it for days. I noticed a large bucket of chalk still outside. Maybe the artist was *still* working.

Then the door to that house banged open, and a kid stepped out. I couldn't believe who it was.

How many ways could Rocco Roman surprise me in one week?

I worried about how to play this. I worried Rocco was going to pound my head into my neck like a Whac-A-Mole just for *looking* at his driveway. But when I see good art, I have to pay the artist a compliment.

Rocco looked genuinely surprised that I liked his artwork.

Then I saw the curtain move at Riley's house, so I hurried away.

Riley was waiting at the front door. As soon as I got inside her house—a perfectly *normal* house, with no butler or twisty slide or bathtub full of Skittles—she had some questions.

Then Riley's mom came around the corner with a tray of treats. This isn't anything new. When we were little, Mrs. Miller was always the mom with the treats. Her purse was bottomless. It got so bad that random kids gathered around her for free stuff.

Anyway, Mrs. Miller seemed happy to see me and wanted to make conversation—she started asking me about school. But Riley interrupted.

In the media room—which was just sort of a den with a big TV—Violet was already on the couch. My stomach did a little flip when I saw her. Violet looked away and sighed deeply, like she couldn't believe I was there.

And then Riley goes:

I had a plan.

I reached into my backpack. The girls recoiled like I was going to pull out a live frog—but hey, I don't want to touch frog guts, either. Instead, I'd come up with a solution. See, every year for Christmas, instead of getting a new iPad or a game system, my dad buys us educational STEM toys, thinking it's going to make Juice Box and me smarter.

In that box of stuff, I'd found a lifelike frog that you could   "dissect." Except instead of real frog guts, the inside was made of plastic and tubes. It was still in the box. It hadn't even been opened.

I told Riley and Violet that we could label the toy frog's intestines and show how the blood pumps in and out of a frog's heart. All without touching a *real frog*.

I pulled it out of the box. I held my breath as they inspected it carefully.

Slime for the win!

THE BONE GAME

Dear Cosmo,

After my great slime win, the Science Fair planning session went . . . okay, I guess. Which is better than how I *thought* it would be—a complete disaster. I mean, Violet and Riley did the entire poster by themselves—even though I'm a better artist with neater handwriting. And they didn't really talk to me, but they didn't make fun of me, either.

There was also the incident with the sparkling water. I'd wanted *normal* water, but Riley said that *all* the fifth graders were drinking sparkling, and it was the cool thing to do. So I decided to give it a try.

Bad idea. I'd never had sparkling before, and I didn't realize it was quite so fizzy.

Luckily, Riley was in the bathroom at the time. Violet looked a little disgusted, but Mrs. Miller got a towel and said it was no big deal.

So we'll just pretend that didn't happen.

But then, when we were leaving, this really surprising thing happened. Violet and I got out to the sidewalk at the same time, and Riley went back inside her house. Violet suddenly turned to me and asked if I wanted to walk home with her. I couldn't believe it.

When we started walking down the sidewalk, I was quiet. My brain was coming up with random thoughts and words. I was so worried I'd say something that made no sense.

Rocco wasn't in his driveway anymore, but his art looked incredible. I'm surprised Violet didn't say anything about it. Actually, she was more interested in my phone. I'd pulled it out to tell my mother I was walking home and I didn't need her to pick me up.

I tried to say the little finger thing just like how Riley said it about *her* mom, but I'm not sure it came out quite right.

Then Violet stopped short, looked down, and gasped. I couldn't believe what she said next.

The Bone Game was this thing we used to play. We tried not to step on sidewalk cracks. If we did, we had to choose which one of our bones we'd be okay with breaking.

I always made up bones that weren't real. I was afraid that if I said a *real* bone, I'd jinx myself, and it would actually happen. So I said things like earlobe bone and stomach bone. It always made Violet giggle.

Did I dare play the Bone Game with her now? But then, *she's* the one who brought it up.

And then we were laughing! *Laughing and playing the Bone Game!* Like old times!

It was so nice. It also made me think of my conversation with Mrs. Hines . . . and what Mrs. Hines wanted me to talk to Violet about.

I don't know what got into me. But suddenly, I was just asking.

I had no idea what she was talking about. I mean—yes—I realize I worry. But why is *that* a reason not to talk to someone?

Not worrying. Yeah right. Not possible.

No one had said this to me before. Not my mom, not my dad, not a teacher—definitely no other friend. It felt like Violet was picking on the fact that I had brown hair, or my shoe size—something I could never change, not if my life depended on it. Worrying was a *part* of me. And Violet was supposed to be *okay* with that.

But then I remembered. Violet wasn't my best friend anymore. So I guess she didn't have to be okay with it after all.

My nose felt peppery. I knew I was going to cry. I had a feeling Violet sensed it because she turned awkwardly and walked down the sidewalk. Without me.

Stepping, I noticed, on all of the cracks.

BEING BRAVE

Dear Cosmo,

Well, it happened. Juice Box got croup again. And just like always, it struck late at night, waking all of us up.

My mom did the tricks she always tried at home to help Juice Box breathe: running a hot shower to steam up the bathroom, sticking his head into the freezer, trying to get him to take deep breaths. But none of it worked, so it was off to the emergency room.

As we were leaving, my dad said this weird thing to my mom.

Mom didn't fool me. There was no big cake. I would have noticed the baking supplies in the cupboard.

This reminded me of the time Mom let me wear her favorite hat to our town's swimming pool, and I lost it. I didn't want to tell her I lost her hat, though, because she'd made me promise over and over that I *wouldn't leave the hat behind*.

So I made something up. And the lie got worse and worse.

At the emergency room, Juice Box got a big welcome from everyone.

They put us in exam room C, which we'd been in plenty of times. As usual, these strange hospital items were there. I notice them every time we come.

I think pee goes in here

The doctor came in and gave Juice Box his medicine and juice. When she was leaving, she turned to me.

You are being so BRAVE and MATURE. Most kids get really NERVOUS in the ER!

I explained that I wasn't the one who was sick. But she said that didn't matter. Often, it was the siblings who *weren't* sick who got more nervous.

I *was* being a brave sibling, I guess. Then again, Juice Box gets croup all the time. It's not scary anymore. But . . . the doctor also said I was being *mature*. Which is the opposite of a *baby*. So if you worry, you're a baby—is that it? Violet said I should stop worrying so much. She also seemed to think certain things were for babies now. Maybe there really is a connection.

I wondered what might happen if I really *did* worry less. Would I be more mature? Would I be cool? Would Violet *like me* again?

Except . . . I wasn't sure I could totally shut my worrying off. I mean, the doctor wasn't even completely correct when she said I was being brave. Sure, I was being brave about Juice Box, but there was a patient in the ER hallway who was making me very nervous.

Maybe I could learn to *control* my worrying, though? Maybe it's like a lamp I could flick on or off. In private, I could turn my worry lamp on, and it could shine as bright as I wanted. Around other people, maybe I could turn the worry lamp off—or at least keep it kind of dim. Maybe I could fake that I wasn't worried at all.

I liked the idea of a worry lamp. I pictured it as this huge sheep lamp our grandma got Juice Box for his birthday.

Okay, then. I'm going to control my worrying. I'll be cool and mature. Starting . . . now.

(But what if it doesn't work? What if I forget to worry about something important, and then something goes wrong? What if I bottle up my worries and I . . . explode?)

Oops. Do-over. Starting . . . *now*.

COOL AS A CUCUMBER

Dear Cosmo,

After spending half the night in the ER, my mom let me sleep in and go into school late. By the time I got there, I was ready to put my plan into action. I was going to keep my worry lamp OFF. I would be as cool as a cucumber.

I don't get that expression, by the way. Is it true that cucumbers are super relaxed compared to other foods?

I wondered what worry would pop up at school first. Maybe I'd have to sharpen my pencil.

But all my pencils were sharp enough. As it turned out, my next challenge was something totally unexpected. It happened just as the lunch bell rang. Mrs. Dunphy announced that we would sit with our Science Fair groups at lunch so we could talk about our projects.

A lot of people groaned, including Riley and Violet. Oh no. Were they groaning because we had to do school stuff during lunch . . . or were they groaning because they had to sit with *me*? Also, this meant I had to stay at school for lunch today.

See, lunch has been a little tricky for me lately. After the first few days of the school year, I wasn't sure if Violet wanted to sit with me anymore, and I didn't want to go into the cafeteria and find out. So I've been using my new phone to call Mom and have her pick me up during the lunch hour. Since our school is a walking district and all the families live close by, you're allowed to leave for lunch as long as a parent signs you out. And as long as you come back for class in the afternoon, of course.

But I haven't left for lunch since second grade—when I met Violet. I've always wanted to stay at school and eat with her. So I've had to give Mom a lot of excuses for why I suddenly want to come home.

It's not like I can tell her the *real* reason, after all. I can just see how *that* would go.

Speaking of Mom—and excuses—*she* didn't have a good excuse for why she suddenly WASN'T baking that big cake for the bake sale.

I've been tracking her on my phone's app, too, but nothing useful has come up. Unless, of course, my mom's secret involves shopping.

Anyway. Back to lunch. The point is, I was hoping to go home today again. But I'm going to try not to worry about it. I have to show Violet I'm cool.

My class tramped to the cafeteria. As a dog, you'd probably like our cafeteria, Cosmo. So many smells! So many crumbs! But for a kid—especially a kid with a worry lamp—it's not all chicken nuggets and tiny cartons of chocolate milk. My cafeteria is crowded, food is always flying, and it's as noisy as a rock concert. I also noticed these troubling things today.

Mysterious puddle   Overflowing trash   Choking is terrifying

It also doesn't help that the third-grade band practices in the cafeteria during lunch.

Still, I tried to ignore all of this as I sat down next to Riley and Violet. For the first minute or so, it went fine. I didn't trip as I sat down in my chair. I didn't spill my juice pouch. But then I saw what

else was in the lunch my mom had packed for me: a slice of my mom's homemade banana bread.

I love my mom's banana bread. But she only bakes it for special occasions. *Actually,* she only bakes it when she feels BAD for me and wants to cheer me up.

Penny needs BOOSTER SHOTS

It's raining on the last day of summer

Someone drew all over Penny's doll

It felt like a banana-bread-shaped sign. This *had* to do with Mom's secret. She felt guilty. My parents are totally getting a divorce. Or maybe she's dying? Maybe that's why she needs her rest?

I tried to keep it together. Maybe it didn't mean anything. Sometimes banana bread is just banana bread, right?

I moved to take a bite. But suddenly, my fingers slipped.

I was in shock. *Banana bread. On the floor.*

At that moment, Rocco Roman walked by. I guess he saw me staring at the banana bread, because he leaned down to pick it up.

Actually, Rocco was wrong. The five-second rule is a total lie. I did that as my topic for the Science Fair in third grade, and I learned that some bacteria can latch onto food *instantly.*

My worry lamp was on full power.

I could feel Violet and Riley watching me. I knew I didn't *have* to eat the banana bread. But I felt overwhelmed, suddenly. Like I couldn't handle *anything.* All the stress with my mom, and now all of the germs on my lunch, and the pressure of sitting with Riley and Violet . . . it was all too much.

So I couldn't help it, Cosmo. I got up, and I ran out of the room.

STOP SIGNS

Dear Cosmo,

I knew where I needed to go: Mrs. Hines's office. She would understand.

I knocked on her door. But then someone who wasn't Mrs. Hines stepped out of the office. Someone . . . *unexpected.*

Mrs. Wink. The crossing guard. She told me that she was stepping in for Mrs. Hines for a little bit. *She* would be the substitute Feelings Teacher!

This was a disaster. There was no way I was going to talk to someone who used a mini stop sign *indoors*. I needed to talk to someone I knew already. Someone I was certain, absolutely *certain*, wouldn't make fun of me when I told her about my worries.

I told Mrs. Wink that, actually, I was feeling pretty good all of a sudden, and I didn't need her help after all. I don't know if she believed me, but she eventually turned her stop sign to the "Go" side and let me leave. Then she walked back into Mrs. Hines's office and shut the door.

I didn't know what to do. I didn't want to go back to the cafeteria. I was sure Violet and Riley would laugh at me.

Back in the hallway, I noticed someone close by. Rocco Roman. I tensed up. Had he come out of the cafeteria to tease me about the banana bread?

But I noticed Rocco didn't have a nasty look on his face. Actually, he looked kind of sad.

Then Rocco tried to get around me to go into Mrs. Hines's office. I decided I should warn him.

I was surprised Rocco got so offended. It didn't *seem* like the wrong thing to say.

But then Rocco said something even more surprising.

Then he looked down at his fists and my scared face and said he was sorry.

I had no idea Rocco had those feelings, though. And I definitely had no idea Rocco didn't know what to say to people. But I also understood. Completely.

Like me, Rocco seemed stunned that Mrs. Hines was out of town. He was so upset that he slid down and sat on the floor. It seemed mean to leave him alone, so I slid down to sit next to him.

Well, I kind of hovered. There was no way I was actually going to touch that dirty floor if I didn't have to.

We sat there for a while. We didn't really say anything, but that was okay. It was kind of nice, honestly. Just being there with Rocco, both of us feeling abandoned together—it made me feel a little better.

MOMS HAVE BAD DAYS, TOO

Dear Cosmo,

I've read that dogs are extra sensitive to their owner's emotions. But if that's true, why didn't you warn me ahead of time that Mom was in a grouchy mood this morning? I could have prepared myself.

I knew Mom was going to put her foot down about me coming home for lunch at some point.

I just wish it didn't happen one day after the Banana Bread Incident.

Speaking of which, I asked Mom about it, but she said she just made banana bread because she had old bananas. Nothing more.

I didn't know what to think about *that.*

Anyway, I stressed about staying at school for lunch all morning. By the time the lunch bell rang, I was feeling really shaky. I was certain that the moment I got to the cafeteria, people were going to remember what happened yesterday, and I'd be the center of attention.

I hesitated in the cafeteria doorway as kids streamed around me. There were a few empty tables toward the back I could sit at, except then I'd be sitting *alone*. And everyone would *see* I was sitting alone, and they'd think I had no friends. Which at this point was kind of true, but I didn't want people to know that.

I could feel my worry lamp shining brightly. I closed my eyes and pictured twisting the knob to dim it a little. It's just lunch. I would be okay.

Then I felt a hand on my arm.

I haven't seen you in here! Wanna sit together?

I've never been so happy to see Maria in my life.

She led me to one of the empty back tables.

After a minute, Kristian sat down, too. Which was great! I even peeked over at Violet and Riley's table, and I noticed Violet glance over. I looked away fast. I told myself that if I just pretended Violet and Riley weren't there, I'd be fine.

Except then Maria and Kristian both looked at me with sneaky smiles.

I wasn't sure what *that* meant. What if Maria and Kristian were famous for starting food fights? What if they did a flash mob dance routine every lunch period? I hoped not. I hated dancing in front of people.

Then Maria pulled a box from her backpack.

Oh dear. Jelly Yum, Jelly Yuck is a popular game at school. Basically, you have a bunch of jelly beans, and then you spin this little wheel that tells you which color of bean you have to choose from the box and eat. Some of the jelly beans taste great, but some of them taste awful, and they're the same color as the good-tasting ones, and you don't know which is which until you put the bean in your mouth. *You* probably wouldn't have an issue with the game, Cosmo, because you eat anything. But I try to stay away from Jelly Yum, Jelly Yuck.

Maria and Kristian got right to it.

Kristian lucked out and got cotton candy. Good for him.

Then it was my turn. I didn't want to go. I think Maria sensed I wasn't so sure because she gave me a tip.

It worked! My bean might have tasted like old pizza, but because I was holding my nose, it wasn't nearly as stinky. It was so much fun!

Rocco came over and played a round. He *didn't* know the hold-your-nose trick, and he made the funniest face when he ate a bean that was dog food instead of lemon meringue pie.

Also, I'm not totally sure about this, but I think Riley and Violet were watching. I didn't look at them, though, because I wasn't sure if they were impressed or making fun.

This afternoon, Mom picked me up after school as usual. She started talking the moment I got into the back seat.

WALLY WOODCHUCK
WORLD OF WOW!

Dear Cosmo,

I really don't understand why you are so obsessed with people food. Like, when there's a waffle on the counter, maybe just leave it there? Because when you eat it, Juice Box gets upset, and then Mom gets mad, and then you get sent outside in the cold.

Anyway, after you got yelled at for eating the waffle, we had to get a move on, because today is Juice Box's birthday party. It isn't Juice Box's birthday. He was born on Christmas Day, and Christmas is always busy. So my parents just let him have a party earlier in the year to make up for it.

This year, he chose to have his party at Wally Woodchuck World of Wow!

Don't get me wrong. I love my little brother. I want him to have a fun birthday party. But I do not like Wally Woodchuck World of Wow!

Here's why:

1. It's filled with arcade games that don't seem to ever get cleaned. One time, I found a chewed glob of gum next to a joystick. Just sitting there.

2. Every half hour, this annoying song plays, and these animatronic animals appear from behind a curtain and start singing. It's a wood-

chuck (Wally), a goldfish (Buster Boo), and then this half-chicken, half-snake thing whose name I forget. If that's not weird enough, the place also has these extra random characters that walk around, too.

Gloopy   Cone Man   This Guy

3. There's a ball pit. This is actually Juice
   Box's favorite part of Wally Woodchuck
   World of Wow!, which makes me wonder
   if the two of us are truly related. I'm so
   afraid of ball pits, I won't even read the
   articles about how dirty they are. They
   call them *PITS* for a reason.

Anyway. Juice Box invited a few of his friends
from preschool. My mom said I could invite some
friends, too. She hinted that maybe Violet could
come, that she hadn't seen Violet around lately
and what was that about?

There was no way I was asking Violet to
World of Wow for obvious reasons. I wondered if
Kristian or Maria would want to come ... but my
worry lamp pinged. What if they laughed? What
if they said World of Wow was for babies? I didn't
think they would, but you never know.

At the same time, I really wanted to hang
out with some friends. Maybe my new friends.
So I tried to put aside my worries. Yesterday
morning, I found Maria and Kristian outside

Mrs. Hines's office, and I worked up my courage and asked.

Have I mentioned I'm terrible at inviting people places?

Maria said she'd love to . . . but she had to study for the Spelling Bee. My first thought was that Maria was lying. She didn't have to study for the Bee! She just didn't want to come to World of Wow! Maybe she thought I was a big worrying baby, just like Violet did!

But maybe I was overthinking things. Maria is a really nice person. She doesn't seem like the type to lie. Maybe I should trust she's telling me the truth.

And then Kristian said he'd be up for it.

I used to love World of Wow! So nostalgic...

Which made me feel great. I was so glad I'd asked after all. See, I'd let go of worrying—a little—and did something scary—and now I had a friend at World of Wow! I felt like my anti-worrying project was working.

Which brings us to today.

My family got to World of Wow right on time. The bright lights were flashing. Kids were screaming. I swear that same glob of gum was still on that same arcade machine.

Then Juice Box's friends arrived, and so did Kristian. To Juice Box's delight, Kristian brought him a gift. I'd mentioned to Kristian that Juice Box is really into Monster Jam. Apparently, Kristian used to be into Monster Jam when he was little as well, and he had a whole bunch of super-rare old trucks in his closet that Juice Box didn't have.

Heard you liked MONSTER JAM, too! So nostalgic...

Kristian seems to think a lot of things are nostalgic.

After that, Kristian and I played Skee-Ball and all the arcade games that didn't have wads of gum on their controllers. Then we sang and had birthday cake. The World of Wow B team was out and about, as usual.

After cake, everyone was really hyper from the sugar. Then I heard Kristian calling out from behind me.

I was terrified for him

in that ball pit. I didn't understand how he could just paddle around in there like it was totally fun and safe.

I mean, it *did* look fun. Kind of. Like, if you ignored the germs.

Could I go in?

I stared into the ball pit. I could practically see the bacteria crawling around. But I needed to be brave. So I took a deep breath, and . . .

It smelled like puke. The balls were slippery in a way that didn't seem right. I got out immediately. Then I used hand sanitizer on my hands and arms and even a little bit on my face until my mom told me that it would probably irritate my skin.

But I did it! And I didn't die!

FRIENDLY NEIGHBORHOOD WORRY-FREE GIRL

Dear Cosmo,

You know how in Spider-Man, Peter Parker gets bitten by a mutant spider, and then he gets all of these superpowers like climbing walls and shooting webs out of his fingers? Well, probably not, because dogs don't watch Marvel movies. But that's kind of how I felt after going in the ball pit. Like there was something *in* that ball pit that transformed me a little.

Not that I plan on going in ball pits again anytime soon.

Well, that's something I don't need to know.

25 Reasons You Should AVOID BALL PITS!!

But you wouldn't believe the worries I've pushed through this week. Like, they're still huge worries, but I've done a good job sort of pretending that they aren't—just like I did with the ball pit. Fake it till you make it, right? It's almost like I don't even need Mrs. Hines anymore.

Well. I probably do still need Mrs. Hines. I mean, I definitely don't want Mrs. Wink as the Feelings Teacher. I don't think anyone does.

Anyway. On Monday, I walked right up to Rocco Roman to tell him something. I was secretly worried he'd laugh, but I didn't let it stop me.

I assured Rocco that he'd like Art Club. So he came. He drew a very accurate picture of a leopard. Everyone was impressed.

Then, on Tuesday, Maria and I went over to Kristian's house. It turns out he only lives a few streets away from me—he says he bikes by my house on the way to the playground all the time. We hung out in the gazebo in his backyard. It's right next to the woods.

I was really nervous at the idea of the howling creature in the woods, but I pretended that I didn't believe Kristian, either.

On Wednesday, I discovered my mom doing this after school:

My first instinct was to worry that eating a huge bowl of ice cream at 3:15 p.m. might be a sign of a weird illness I'd never heard of. Mom is always telling Juice Box and me that ice cream is only for special occasions, and that if we ate it in the afternoon, we'd spoil our dinner.

Then again, parents do a lot of confusing things. So I decided to ignore the worry and walk away.

And then there's my Science Fair group. This week, Mrs. Dunphy had us work on our projects in class. On Thursday, Riley somehow got permission for us to work in the hallway.

When we got out there, I think I played it pretty cool.

I quickly found out the real reason the girls wanted to work in the hall.

At least that hasn't changed. Violet has had a crush on Zack Washington since they got paired to make gingerbread houses for the second-grade Holiday Fair. But she's never been brave enough to write him a note.

Instead of working on the project, Violet started her letter to Zack.

As soon as it came out of my mouth, my worry lamp flashed. Why didn't I just keep my mouth shut? Riley wouldn't like it that I disagreed with her suggestion.

Violet looked at Riley, and Riley shrugged. Then Violet started writing. I decided to mind my own business and not ask any more questions after that. Then the girls tiptoed around the corner to Zack's locker. I didn't have time to worry about getting in trouble as the lookout, because they were back only a few seconds later.

Riley and Violet giggled for the rest of the time we were in the hall. I pretended it didn't bother me. I just worked on my part of the project.

But Cosmo, like I was saying about suddenly having superpowers from the ball pit? I really do think I've transformed. Because then *this* happened on Friday.

I couldn't believe they were inviting me. Was it because I was acting less worried? Maybe Violet noticed? So . . . now would we be friends again? That would be amazing—instead of having no friends, I'll have lots!

I have to be very careful, though. I can't show any signs of worry at this sleepover. I can't just keep my worry lamp dim. I have to leave it at *home*.

Here goes nothing, Cosmo. Wish me luck.

THE SLEEPOVER

Dear Cosmo,

It probably comes as no surprise that I have a hard time with sleepovers. I've had a lot of false starts through the years.

It's just that everyone's house is so different from mine. I don't know where the parents' bedrooms are. There are unfamiliar noises at night. And then there was Violet's older brother, Will, who thought scaring girls was funny.

I've gotten used to sleeping at Violet's house, though. (It also helped when I realized *Will* was the ghost.) Luckily, that's where the sleepover was tonight.

I'm glad it wasn't at Riley's house. I didn't really dwell on it at the time, but when we went to Riley's to do the Science Fair stuff, I'd noticed there was a cuckoo clock in her kitchen.

Cuckoo clocks make me nervous. What does the cuckoo do when he's inside the clock for that whole hour? Nothing? *Really?*

Anyway. I got to Violet's house at seven sharp, just like Riley said. Mrs. Vance opened the door, and she was really happy to see me.

I didn't want to hug her *too* long, though, because Violet and Riley might think that was weird. Still, it was nice to be missed.

Violet's mom told me the girls were upstairs. I could hear music playing and Riley and Violet laughing. My heart started to pound. I knew what Violet and I did at our sleepovers, but what was it going to be like with Riley around? Were we going to have to talk about our future prom dates? Were we going to drink coffee and watch R-rated movies? I wasn't sure I could handle that.

But when I went into Violet's room, the girls were standing in front of Violet's closet, which had been kind of transformed. There was a ton of CANDY in there now.

We grabbed at stuff. I picked a huge pack of minty gum and some sour worms. Over the next half hour, I ate the entire package of sour worms, and Violet ate a giant peanut butter chocolate bar, and Riley poured straight sugar from Pixy Stix into her mouth.

We got kind of hyper after that. But in a good way!

I could totally handle a dance party. That's what Violet and I did at our *normal* sleepovers.

Then Riley had another idea. She brought out a huge plastic case of makeup and hair stuff that she'd brought from home. Violet squealed, but I wasn't so sure. I'm really not a makeover person.

Riley said they should do me FIRST. Violet agreed. I tried to swallow down my worries. I didn't want to mess up this sleepover.

But actually, it wasn't so bad.

When they were finished, Violet took pictures of us with her instant camera. I was happy she was still using it because I'd given it to her for her birthday last year. And also—she was taking pictures of us, *together.*

I was starting to relax. Maybe I'd been wrong about Riley. She was being okay! The sleepover was shockingly normal!

But then it all changed, Cosmo. Because this happened.

TRUTH OR DARE

Dear Cosmo,

Be glad dogs don't have to play Truth or Dare and that the dog next door will never come up to you and make you either tell a secret or do a stunt.

Because it's ALL VERY STRESSFUL.

I was really hoping Violet would say she didn't want to play. She and I had never played Truth or Dare at sleepovers. In fact, I remember a sleepover last year where we both agreed the game was dumb. No such luck.

The game started out okay, I guess.

I'll go first!

Wait. Did Riley mean Michael *McMinnamin*, the kid I had gotten stuck with for Math Relay Race? Huh.

Still. I could handle this. Maybe we'd just talk about random boys and eat spoonfuls of spices.

But then it was my turn. I really, *really* didn't want to choose dare. I was afraid that it would set off my worry lamp. So I chose truth.

Big mistake.

I didn't want to talk about my new friends. And I definitely didn't want to give away that they most likely met in Mrs. Hines's waiting room. I had no idea if they wanted people to know they talked to the Feelings Teacher.

Could I skip my turn? Or say I wanted another question?

I knew I couldn't. They'd say I was a baby. And I noticed Violet watching me like she really wanted me to get this right. I really, *really* wanted to be friends with Violet again. And Riley, too, I guess, because now they seemed like they came as a package.

The girls perked up like they knew I was going to say something juicy. But I stopped myself before I could say anything else.

Then Violet and Riley had *more questions.*

That wasn't fair. Violet knew there wasn't anything in Mr. Howdy's beard. It was just a dumb rumor. But it wasn't the answer they wanted. So I said I'd heard there were worms living in there. I also even laughed—a little—when Riley said Art Club was for babies. My heart hurt, though, because I didn't want Art Club to be for babies. I liked it too much.

Thankfully, Mrs. Vance called for us right then, saying she'd made some popcorn. We all got up to go downstairs. My legs felt heavy, and it wasn't because I'd been sitting on a deflated beanbag for a while. It was because I'd sat on a deflated beanbag and listened to Violet and Riley cut up people I liked. And I hadn't defended them. Worse, I'd sort of *agreed*.

As we were heading down the stairs, Riley turned and looked at me.

Violet was grinning at me like this was all great. Which . . . it *was* great, I guess. I wanted Violet as my friend again. I wanted to sit with her at lunch, just like last year. I wanted things back to normal.

Then Violet pulled me aside and whispered one more thing.

And I have to say, that felt really, really good, too.

Mostly.

I BEFORE E

Dear Cosmo,

Over the past few days, my worry lamp has really been blinking. I want to be friends with everyone. Violet for sure . . . but Maria, Kristian, and Rocco, too. But Riley doesn't want that, and if I upset Riley, I'll lose Violet. It's a lot to handle.

But so far, it's been going okay, so I'm not sure why I'm worried.

Like the lunch thing. All I had to say to Maria was this:

I didn't like telling her a white lie, but it wasn't like I could tell Maria that Riley specifically didn't want me to sit with her and the others.

That would be mean.

Then Violet invited me over without Riley this week to finish up the Science Fair project. I read her what I'd prepared to say for our presentation. She said it was great! Then we made stuff out of our favorite baking clay. I made a cool Halloween pumpkin pin. Violet made a weird creature with a long tongue and antennas.

It was a lot of fun, even though occasionally Violet seemed to notice she was having too much fun or something, because then she made what I call a "Riley face."

I still wanted to do Art Club, too. Though . . . I kind of had to creep into Art Club when Violet and Riley weren't looking.

I know I shouldn't care. *I* don't think Art Club is for babies. But, well, I also don't want them to make fun of me.

I've missed seeing my other friends at lunch, so Kristian, Maria, Rocco, and me have been meeting secretly in the music room when we're supposed to have appointments with Mrs. Wink. Mostly, we just gossip about how strange Mrs. Wink is. We also play Uno and look at graphic novels, and Kristian used the program he created to come up with roller coaster nicknames for all of us.

So it seems like maybe I *can* handle all these friends. And yet I'm still so worried. I mean, yesterday afternoon, I was so uneasy that I chewed a bunch of the mint gum I'd taken from Violet's candy stash! You were there, Cosmo. You wanted to chew something, too.

But this morning, I finally figured out what was going on. When I got to school, I found Maria standing on the school stairs, staring at a long list of words. Then I remembered: The Spelling Bee is today! Of *course* I've been worried—I knew Maria was worried about it. I knew exactly what *that* felt like.

I went over a list of spelling rules with Maria to keep her sharp.

At that moment, a bunch of kids climbed the stairs toward the front door, including Riley. She saw Maria and me and said hi, but her smile was kind of weird, like she'd swallowed a bug.

Then Maria said something surprising.

I asked Maria what she meant, and she shrugged, saying she didn't like talking about people. Boy, did *that* start my worry lamp glowing. But I tried to turn it off. I wasn't the Penny who worried anymore. Everything was going well! I needed to relax!

In class later, Mrs. Dunphy said we were doing another Math Relay Race. For the second time, she picked Michael McMinnamin and me to be partners.

Just before we got started, a note landed on my desk. I turned around. Riley was smiling at me. Whoa. Riley, sending *me* a note?

I looked at the folded piece of paper she'd just sent . . . and over at my Math Relay Race partner. I suddenly remembered what Riley said about Michael during Truth or Dare.

Oh dear. Had Riley passed me a note about *Michael McMinnamin*?

But then I opened the piece of paper and saw what she wrote.

After school, as in *today*? But the Spelling Bee was today. I'd promised Maria I'd go. I couldn't let her down.

I could tell Riley was waiting for me to write a response. I had to come up with *something*.

I'd only fudged the truth a little. My parents *are* hiding something. But I had no idea when they were going to tell me about it. Anyway, I couldn't tell Riley about the Bee because I knew it would make her mad. I was choosing my other friends over her. And I knew that if I made Riley mad, I might lose Violet as a friend again.

So I just figured this would be easier. It's not like Riley would ever *know* I'd deceived her, right?

Oh, and by the way, it's all thanks to Maria that I know how to spell *deceived* in the first place. *I* before *E*, except after *C*. Some examples are *piece, relieve,* and *believe.*

And also the word *lie.*

HYPERLEXIC ORTHOGRAPHERS

Dear Cosmo,

The Spelling Bee was held in our multi-purpose room, which is exactly what it sounds like: a room where lots of different events happen.

Kindergarten Pageant   Charity Contests   Giant Jenga Club

There were chairs set up on the stage for the spellers. There were also lots of family members already in the audience. Some families went all out. This girl Samantha brought both sets of grandparents and a bunch of cousins.

We were a pretty good cheering section for Maria, too.

Classical music started to play, and the kids competing in the Spelling Bee walked onto the stage. Maria looked *so nervous*. I could relate. I can't even *get* on a stage without shaking.

The person running the Bee was Mrs. Pollard, the school librarian. Which makes sense, because Mrs. Pollard is always using huge words that no one knows the meaning of.

The competition started. A few kids were eliminated right away.

Maria hung in there, though, through the first round, and then the second, and then the third! Whenever she got a word correct, we cheered. She kept looking to the corner of the room to these two people in the audience. I wondered if one of them was her older sister—the one

188

Maria said had won the Bee when she was Maria's age.

Finally, the only kids left were Maria and this kid Paolo, who has almost as good a vocabulary as Mrs. Pollard. My worry lamp was really flashing for Maria. She looked so scared.

Then, right before it was Maria's turn to spell again, I noticed someone out the window.

How could Riley be *here*? She was supposed to be at her house, eating killer snacks. But when I looked again, Riley wasn't outside anymore. Maybe I hadn't seen her at all.

So I turned to the stage again. It was Maria's turn. I crossed my fingers for her.

I couldn't believe it. Maria never made mistakes!

It was still and silent in the multipurpose room. Even Mrs. Pollard seemed shocked. But then she got it together and turned to Paolo, the only kid left.

Okay, *poultice*? *Ziggurat*? Are these even real words?

Paolo seemed to think so, because according to Mrs. Pollard, he spelled *poultice* correctly.

Meaning . . . Maria had *lost!*

Everyone started cheering, and balloons dropped from the ceiling, and Mrs. Pollard walked over to give Paolo the bee-shaped hat.

Maria shook his hand like a good sport, but then she ran off behind the stage. And didn't come out. I turned to my friends.

I'd never been behind the multipurpose room's curtain before, and when we got back there, I didn't like how dark it was. I also saw a huge spiderweb in the corner that I tried my best to ignore.

Then we heard a tiny sound in the corner.

It was Maria. She sounded really upset.

I was nervous as Rocco walked over to Maria. His fists were clenched. He had a big frown. I was worried he might punch the wall or something.

We watched as Rocco stood over Maria's chair. A long moment passed.

Maria looked startled. Then she started laughing. Then cried again.

But we thought that was ridiculous.

The curtains rustled. It was Maria's mom and sister. When Maria saw them, she started crying again. They rushed over to her.

Maria's sister went on to say that if *she'd* been in this year's Spelling Bee, she would have been out after the third round. Also, neither Maria's mom nor her sister had any clue what a ziggurat was anyway. Coming in second, they both said, was something to be very proud of. Life wasn't *always* about winning.

THE SCIENCE FAIR

Dear Cosmo,

Well, today is the day. The Science Fair. Finally. But I feel ready. I've practiced what I was going to say in front of the mirror so many times, I have my speech memorized.

Instead of having a normal morning at school, everyone started setting up their projects and preparing their speeches. Maria gave my hand a quick squeeze in the hallway. She knew I didn't like speaking in public.

The Science Fair took place in the gym. When I got there, I looked around the room at the other projects and posters. It didn't seem like anyone else had done the frog's digestive system.

But even though I was feeling as cool as a cucumber—well, mostly—Riley was acting sort of . . . weird. She was really quiet as she set up the poster. And every time she looked at me, she kept making Riley faces.

Which, I mean, she *is* Riley. Of course she's going to make Riley faces. But her faces seemed *extra* Riley today. I was so uneasy about it, I asked Violet.

But Violet didn't answer.

Was it *me*? Did I smell like the blueberry waffle I'd had for breakfast? Did I have dog hair all over me? But everything *seemed* fine. I didn't understand what was wrong.

The room filled up. I even noticed Mrs. Hines come in. She was back! She spotted me across the room.

I was so happy to see her! And people really liked our project. And though I stumbled a few times during my speech, Mrs. Dunphy seemed pleased.

I was happy it was all over. Thrilled, actually, because I'd been worrying about it for so long!

But when I turned around, Riley and Violet weren't smiling. They were whispering. Then I noticed they were looking over my shoulder. When I turned around, I saw that Maria, Kristian, and Rocco were heading over to see our frog.

That's when Riley got this strange expression—not quite the Riley face—almost like she was about to laugh, but not a *nice* laugh. And even though she hadn't spoken to me all morning, she started talking in this really loud voice, like she hoped the whole room could hear.

So I *had* seen Riley out the window after school yesterday. Uh-oh.

I tried to make an excuse. But Riley talked over me—even *louder* than before.

My heart started to pound. I didn't want my friends to think I was embarrassed! And my other friends definitely heard what Riley was saying, because they stopped and they all looked really hurt.

Then it got even worse.

I hadn't said those things. Not really. I mean, I *had* said Rocco didn't know how to talk to people—but that was because I didn't want Riley to think he was mean. And also, I didn't say he talked to Mrs. Hines! I'd stopped myself!

As I looked over, Rocco looked upset. All my friends did. My heart started pounding. I needed to make this right.

I looked at Violet. She would explain that Riley was twisting everything, right?

Then Violet turned to Riley, and both of them pretended like I wasn't there. This wasn't fair.

I turned to Kristian, Maria, and Rocco. I needed to explain, but what could I say? Maybe if I told the truth, they'd understand?

Or . . . maybe not.

ROCK BOTTOM

Dear Cosmo,

The rest of the morning passed in a haze. I don't remember talking to anyone at the Science Fair, and I don't remember anyone talking to me. I looked around for Mrs. Hines, but she must have left because I didn't see her anywhere. Even weirder, no other adult seemed to notice anything was wrong. Which makes no sense. Adults always notice the littlest things—stuff you don't *want* them to notice—but when something is really wrong, they're all like:

It seems like everyone is having a GREAT DAY!

After the Science Fair was over, I sprinted to Mrs. Hines's room. Luckily, she didn't have another kid in her office right then. She seemed happy to see me. Boy, was *she* in for a surprise.

I burst into tears. I blubbered about the worry lamp, and the ball pit, and my new friends, and Violet inviting me to the sleepover, and then screwing everything up. I told her about the banana bread and the cake my mom never baked and how Riley and Violet had promised, *promised* they wouldn't tell anybody what I said during Truth or Dare but did anyway. And how I was never, *ever* playing Truth or Dare again because I'd hurt some friends I really cared about.

Hmm. I hadn't thought about it that way. I mean, I knew *I* hadn't been a good friend. But then I started to think about if other people had been good or bad friends to *me*.

I thought about Maria squeezing my hand in the hall, telling me I would rock the Science Fair speech. Good friend.

I thought of Rocco apologizing to me outside of Mrs. Hines's office about the banana bread. Good friend.

I thought of Kristian keeping me company at

Juice Box's party and even bringing Juice Box a thoughtful gift. Good friend.

Riley has never been thoughtful.

Riley has never apologized about anything.

Riley would probably never squeeze my hand and tell me I'd be okay.

And . . . I'm not sure if Violet would anymore, either.

And I thought about how Riley said all those things about Maria and Kristian and Rocco in front of them on purpose. To hurt me. But also to hurt them. And Violet just backed her up. She didn't defend me—just like I didn't defend Maria, Kristian, or Rocco. I wondered if Violet felt as guilty as I did right now.

I wondered if she realized what she did to me at all.

A terrible feeling came over me. Violet wasn't a good friend to me anymore. There was no way around it. I was trying so hard to stay friends with her . . . but maybe that made no sense.

Maybe I had to let her go.

A MYSTERY SOLVED

Dear Cosmo,

At lunchtime, I really didn't want to go to the cafeteria. But there was no way I could call Mom again. I'd told her lunch was good now. She'd ask questions I wasn't ready to answer.

I considered hiding in the bathroom. The thing is, at our school, they don't let you do that. We have this aide, Mrs. Root, who regularly checks the bathrooms at different times of the day to make sure kids aren't hiding out.

I also thought about going to the nurse, but I avoided the nurse at all costs. Kids who were actually *sick* hung out in there.

So I had no choice but to go into the cafeteria.

I saw Violet and Riley sitting at their regular table. Violet glanced at me for a second, but then she looked away. It made my heart hurt a little.

Okay, it made my heart hurt a *lot*.

Then I saw Maria, Rocco, and Kristian. They were all sitting together, but they weren't really talking. They kind of looked sad. My heart pounded as I walked to their table.

I tried to explain that I hadn't been thinking clearly and that I should have defended them. But I'd gotten so caught up in keeping Violet as a friend that I changed everything about myself to fit in with her and Riley—including not worrying! I was so worried about not worrying, but the whole time, I *was* worrying—about Violet and Riley letting me hang out with them!

Then I just stood there, not sure what I should do next. They didn't say I *couldn't* sit with them, but I wasn't sure they wanted me there, either.

I heard someone laughing and whispering behind me. It was Riley and Violet. I thought they were laughing and whispering about me, but they weren't looking at me at all. They were looking at someone else.

Petra from Art Club was sitting alone, like she usually does. I could tell she could hear Riley and Violet, but she was pretending not to. I was really annoyed, suddenly. What had Petra ever done to them?

Then I did something that totally surprised me. I walked over to Petra. Right up to her otherwise empty table.

I was worried Riley and Violet might have told Petra I'd said mean things about her, too. Not that I *had*, but we had talked about Art Club at the sleepover. I could see them twisting my words just like they did about Kristian, Maria, and Rocco.

But Petra slid her stuff right over so I could sit.

I could still hear giggling behind me. It was pretty stressful. But then I noticed something written on the notebook on the table, and I forgot all about everything else.

My mouth dropped open. I couldn't believe it.

This was incredibly exciting. I told Petra I sat at the desk that had the Bug Man message written inside! Petra said she wrote that message in the desk last year, when we were in fourth.

And I meant it. I would never tell anyone Petra was Bug Man. I would be the kind of person who kept promises and didn't talk about people behind their backs. The kind of friend you could trust.

I just wished I'd figured that out a few days ago.

GUM

Dear Cosmo,

When I got home from school, I was really sad. Little did I know the day was about to get a whole lot worse.

My mom and Juice Box were sitting in the living room. Juice Box was telling my mom this long story about monster trucks, as usual. As soon as I walked through the front door, my mom jumped up, excited.

I know she was worried about me, but I didn't want to tell her I'd lost all my friends. Sure, I was happy that I'd done the right thing with Petra—and bonded with her about Bug Man. But now I just felt guilty again. And embarrassed and sad because Maria, Rocco, and Kristian would probably never talk to me again.

I went up into my bedroom, figuring I'd draw. Usually drawing makes me feel a little bit better. But then I found you, Cosmo.

You didn't get up to greet me. Your eyes were glazed. Your tail barely thumped. And you were breathing kind of funny. Fast, but also like you were in pain. This wasn't right. I shouted down to my mom.

Maybe I was worrying too much again? I mean, you eat weird things all the time, and you're usually fine. But my worry lamp was really pinging. Then, when I leaned down to give you a kiss, I smelled something suspicious on your breath.

Mint.

See, last year, my Science Fair project was all about foods that were poisonous to dogs. Chocolate is an obvious one—everyone knows about that. But dogs also shouldn't eat onions, grapes, or raisins. And there was something on that list that's very, *very* dangerous to dogs that a lot of people don't know about.

Sugar-free minty gum.

At first, I couldn't think of where you might have found minty gum, Cosmo. But then I remembered: Violet's candy closet. I'd been chewing some the other day. You ate a sock, remember?

I ran to my closet where I kept the gum. The door had been nudged open.

I knew what I had to do. I flew into action.

Luckily, that got my mom's attention. Even luckier, my dad was home early from work. When my dad saw you, he got this really worried look on his face. Both of them were able to carry you down the stairs and into the car, and we all went to the emergency vet.

In the car, it got even scarier.

We got to the animal hospital pretty fast. My dad ran into the office and shouted something to the vets. They brought out a stretcher and put you on it. Your eyes were closed. I could barely see your chest rising. I was crying so hard because I knew I was going to lose you. It was *my gum* you'd eaten, *my fault* you were sick!

The vets took you into a treatment room, but they didn't allow us in. They closed the door. My mom rubbed my shoulder, but it didn't make me feel calm.

A few minutes later, the vet came out and told us the thing I was most afraid to hear.

I'm really worried about Cosmo. We are trying everything...

... but it doesn't look good.

Oh no. Oh *no*. This isn't supposed to happen, Cosmo. The stuff I worry about—*it's not supposed to come true!*

My mom held me close, telling me not to worry, but that made no sense. *Not worrying* had ruined everything. I tried to get Violet to be my friend again by not worrying, and look where it got me. I tried to ignore my flashing worry lamp and trusted Riley, only to be humiliated. I tried not to worry about normal, everyday things, and I'd forgotten that sugar-free mint gum was poisonous to dogs. And while we're on the subject of not worrying, I'd *completely* forgotten about Mom's secret. I probably should have been worrying more about that, too.

I looked at her, wanting to explode.

My mom told me to quiet down. She promised me that everything was fine. But why should I believe *her*? Everything *else* was going wrong.

Just then, the vet called my parents over to talk. I wanted to go, too, but my mom said to stay with Juice Box. They went into a treatment room and shut the door.

My worries spiraled. Every time I heard a beep in the back room, I was afraid it was you, Cosmo, taking your last breath. I'm so sorry, Cosmo. I never meant for this to happen. I love you so much. I should have worried like I always do. I shouldn't have tried to turn my worry lamp off. I should have just been *me*.

I waited for my parents to come out. I waited for the worst-case scenario, the thing I feared most in the world. As I waited, the front door to the vet's office opened.

And I couldn't believe who walked through.

THROUGH THICK AND THIN

Dear Cosmo,

I blinked a few times to make sure I wasn't seeing things. Three people had just walked into the emergency vet's office. Three people I *knew.*

Maria said of course she didn't hate me. Kristian and Rocco agreed—though they both said it wasn't nice I talked about them behind their backs.

They forgave me, they said. That's what friends do.

As far as finding out about what happened with you, Cosmo, remember how I said Kristian lives only a few streets away? He was biking by our house to the park when we were getting you in the car. I had run back inside to get your favorite squeaky hamburger, but Kristian asked my mom what was going on and where we were going—and she said you weren't doing well.

And then Kristian called Maria and Rocco. And they came here, to make sure I was all right.

I was happy for a minute. My friends had forgiven me. They were *here*. But then I remembered you, Cosmo. And I fell apart.

Maria, Kristian, and Rocco said they'd sit with me. My parents were still talking to the vet, so we had no update. But my friends didn't seem to mind waiting. They really helped everyone out.

Finally, my mom and dad came back from talking to the vet. They had serious, scary expressions. The vet had told them that the next half hour of medicine would determine if you made it or didn't, Cosmo. After that, we would know.

There was a huge lump in my throat. I couldn't wait a half hour! That felt like years!

I thought of you on that little stretcher in the hospital room. I was wrong about ball pits being my biggest worry. Or Math Relay Race, or banana bread on the cafeteria floor. *You're* my biggest worry, Cosmo, and none of that other stuff matters.

But I will say, one thing made it a little *less* awful. As the minutes ticked down, my friends moved even closer. They held my hands.

It was quiet inside the treatment room. When the door opened, the vet had a mask on, so I couldn't see his expression. I was sure you were gone, Cosmo. I was sure I'd lost you.

My heart banged so hard as the vet walked over. I tried to be brave. Then the vet pulled off his mask.

Wait. What? I was sure I'd heard him wrong.

Cosmo, you're gonna be okay.

THE SECRET

Dear Cosmo,

First of all, I'm so happy that I can still write this to you. I don't know what I would have done if I had lost you. I'm never going to let that happen. I'm officially no longer chewing gum. Or eating onions, raisins, or chocolate.

Well. Chocolate might be a tough one. But I'm going to keep it far away from you.

The vet wanted to keep you at the hospital overnight to watch over you. I worried all night. What if the vet was wrong about you getting better? What if you took a turn for the worse? What if you woke up and felt confused? You usually slept on my floor or on my bed. Now you were in a cold, dark dog crate, without us. At least you had your favorite squeaky hamburger. I'm glad I remembered to bring it for you.

Then, in the morning, we got this call.

So Dad went and picked you up. When you came home, I was so happy to see you.

You really are my best friend, Cosmo. My best friend in the whole world.

But I started thinking about my *other* best friends—the human kind. It was so special that Maria, Kristian, and Rocco came so quickly to be with me when you were sick. They forgave me, and they were there for me.

Of course, my mom had an opinion about my new friends.

Those kids at the vet seem so NICE.

You can have them over whenever.

Really! Even school nights!

Then I thought about my old best friend. Violet. She never called to talk about what happened at the Science Fair. She also never called to talk about what happened to you, Cosmo. I have a feeling she knows. My mom is still friends with Mrs. Vance, and this morning, we got a delivery from the pet store.

In the old days, Violet would have called me to make sure I was okay. She would have called a whole bunch of times, actually, even if I didn't want to talk. Violet knew you were a special dog. The two of us used to dress you up in costumes and pretend that you were a sea monster on the bed. We were going to create an account for you the moment our moms let us get Instagram.

It still makes me sad. I miss Violet so much. But I guess that sometimes, you have to let friends go. Especially if they aren't being good friends anymore. Especially if they want you to change who you are. Because that's what I've realized: I can't stop being me. It's probably good not to worry so much about *everything* . . . but worrying isn't so bad *all* the time. After all, Cosmo, worrying saved your life.

(By the way, Mrs. Hines didn't tell me any of that stuff. I thought of it *all on my own.*)

Anyway, after I hugged you for a good long while, I realized someone was standing in the doorway, watching me. It was my dad. He had a strange look on his face.

All of a sudden, I knew. *The secret.* There really *was* one. And they were finally going to tell me.

My dad led me to the couch. My legs were shaky. I wasn't sure I wanted to know. I'd already had enough bad news, and everything was okay for a minute. I couldn't take another roller coaster ride.

Then my mom came in. For a few moments, she just stared at me with this little smile on her face that I didn't understand. Then she spat it out.

I made her repeat it a few times. My brain slowly worked to process what she'd said. *Pregnant?* I had some questions.

For *three*? Then my mom told me something even wilder. She's not having one baby. She's having TWO.

Twins? There were going to be *double* the number of kids in this house soon?

Yikes. They said they were telling me this and that they would tell Juice Box soon enough. I wondered how *he* would take it. Juice Box and I had better stick together.

I was so shocked. But it wasn't a bad kind of shock. Babies would be a huge change, but maybe it would be exciting. It will *definitely* be exciting for you, Cosmo—that's double the amount of food dropped on the floor! As long as it's not grapes, onions, chocolate, or gum, of course.

Then I remembered one last thing that had been bothering me. *Monster Jam.* I asked her what she was *really* up to when she didn't go.

Then what were you doing in that random office building?

What's BAREFOOT BABES?

Oh! That's where my Barefoot Babes group meets.

A prenatal yoga group! And actually, don't tell, but one of your classmates' moms is a Barefoot Babe, too!

One of my classmates' moms? *Who?*

I don't know how I knew what she was going to say next, Cosmo. I really don't. But a sinking feeling came over me right then. And when the name came out of my mom's mouth, it was exactly what I had been expecting.

I told my mom not to worry about me telling Riley. *I* knew how to keep a secret. Unlike other people.

But . . . *Riley's mom?* Spending lots of *time* together? With new twin babies . . . *and Riley?*

Think of me fondly, Cosmo. Because this is a challenge I'm really not sure I'll make it through.

EPILOGUE

Dear Cosmo,

Sorry I haven't written much lately. I've been so busy, and most of the drawing I've been doing is in Art Club. I've also been back with Mrs. Hines, and with the secret meetings I still have with Maria, Kristian, and Rocco in the music room, I haven't had as many worries to write about.

But don't get me wrong. I still worry about all kinds of things.

What if a BEE flies into this soda can and I swallow a bee?

Is aluminum poisonous?

What if Mom finds out I'm DRINKING SODA?

But my new friends have really helped. They don't mind me talking about the stuff I worry about. They don't say it's babyish, or boring, or that they want me to be different. Just like I accept that Maria is sometimes too perfect, and Rocco has the urge to punch stuff now and then, and Kristian talks way too much about roller coasters, my friends accept that I'm the worrier of the group. It's just who I am. It makes me *me*.

Oh, and we've been hanging out with Petra a little bit, too. But don't worry. I've kept her secret.

Anyway, speaking of roller coasters: That's where we were today, actually. Kristian finally talked us into joining him at Adventure Land, his favorite amusement park. He got really into planning the day for Maria, Rocco, Petra, and me.

I was really hoping he wouldn't pick the Head Chopper. Even the name is terrifying.

I was surprised when Maria and Rocco agreed pretty quickly to go on the Head Chopper. I knew that Kristian probably wouldn't be mad if I chickened out, but I did feel a little bit better when he gave me a few key stats.

So I got in line with the others. As we were waiting, I noticed some girls near the cotton candy cart. I couldn't believe who it was.

There was someone else with them, too: Lulu McDaniels, also from our grade. The only thing I know about Lulu is that she's really good at lacrosse.

I watched as the three of them walked toward one of the games. Riley and Lulu were in front, and Violet trailed behind them.

Riley was making the Riley face. Maybe I shouldn't have cared,

but Violet looked so . . . *lonely.* I mean, Violet might not be my friend anymore, but I didn't want her to be sad.

So I turned to Maria. She'd already noticed what I was looking at.

I walked over to Violet. At this point, she'd moved over to sitting on a bench by herself. When Violet saw me, she looked kind of embarrassed.

I was surprised when Violet said yes. When she shouted to Riley and Lulu that she'd be back, they didn't even notice.

But I pretended not to notice them not noticing.

We got back in line for the Head Chopper. This was happening nearby, which was a good distraction.

Is it me, or do Sue the Magician and Jimmy the Llama look alike?

But then Sue and her llama moved on. I looked at Violet, and I didn't know what to say. It's so weird—only a few months ago, Violet was my best friend. The *perfect* best friend. Now I feel like I don't know her at all. But I was glad she was joining us on the Head Chopper. I didn't think people should be left alone or made fun of at amusement parks, of all places.

Eventually, we were at the front of the line. We all piled into the cars. My heart was really pounding. I had a last-minute question for the Head Chopper's ride operator.

The guy said that no one had been killed. He promised. Really.

But maybe he just *had* to say that.

Still, I buckled myself in. Violet sat down

next to me. After she made sure her seat belt was secure, she looked over at me.

Then the ride started with a jerk. A chain dragged us up this huge hill that seemed to go on and on. My heart was banging. This seemed *so* unsafe. I couldn't believe I was even on this thing. I wouldn't have tried it a few months ago.

But then, I guess I'm different now. A little, anyway.

Kristian waved his arms in the air. Rocco shouted excitedly. Just like Violet predicted, I kept my eyes firmly closed all the way up the hill. But for one tiny second, at the very top of the hill, I opened them up. I could see the whole park from up there. The parking lot, too, and the roads, and the highway, and even the houses beyond—including *my* house, maybe, though I couldn't really tell.

It was actually kind of . . . incredible.

But then all the worries came back, and I closed my eyes again.

I felt the roller coaster pause at the top. Then I felt the front of the car tipping and falling, falling, flying down the hill. Ahead of me, Kristian screamed. Maria and Rocco yelled. And then I held on for dear life, Cosmo, as we started our terrifying—but maybe a little bit fun—plunge all the way down.

ACKNOWLEDGMENTS

It has been a dream to create Penny. Literally—I have been creating stories with illustrations since I was a kid, and writing something like this has always been something I wanted to do. At the same time, I wasn't sure if I could do it because Penny's voice is so unique and, frankly, I'm not an illustrator! But I want to thank everyone who believed in this project—and who fell in love with Penny as hard as I did. Those people include Lanie Davis, Sara Shandler, Josh Bank, Les Morgenstein, and Romy Golan on the Alloy team—how exciting it was to send off early chapters of Penny in hopes that you got all the jokes! And then my fantastic crew at Putnam: Jen Klonsky, Matt Phipps, Marikka Tamura, and Suki Boynton, who also got exactly what Penny was about and just let her be . . . Penny. (And who were extremely patient when I decided to redraw all of the artwork for this book at least four times over.) Thank you to Michelle Lippold, Jacqueline Hornberger, and Cindy Howle for copyediting and proofreading. And thank you to Richard Abate, too, who helped make all of this happen.

I want to thank those educators who encouraged me from an early age not only to love reading but also to continue drawing: the teachers at Corl Street Elementary in State College, Pennsylvania; the fantastic English staff at Downingtown Senior High School; and Ron Pavlick, my art teacher when I was in tenth grade, whose gentle guidance was inspirational. Thanks also to my sister, Ali, because I most likely borrowed a lot of Penny's expressions from her and her Squall cartoons, especially the one about the giant Plinko board and the cooking competition. And to my parents, Mindy and Shep, who provided a lot of the jokes in this book without even realizing it, like the Easter Bunny without his vest.

Thank you to Clara and Max McGarry-Grubb (and mom Colleen!) not only for reading this novel early but also for helping me out with cover ideas! Clara and Max, I think you might write books someday, too! And a big thank-you to Christie Ketterman, the school psychologist at Markham Elementary, who read an early draft and provided good advice on what the "Feelings Teacher" would actually say to Penny when her worry lamp was shining the brightest. Thanks to Jocelyn Artinger, Markham's principal, for being so supportive. Thank you to my favorite worriers, Michael and Henry, for being exactly who you are and knowing when you need to talk to your own Feelings Teachers. Thank you to Kristian, who inspired the Kristian in this book and corrected me on some roller coaster mistakes. Thank you to Clyde, who was the inspiration for Cosmo—including the part about eating the gum. All of that is true, including the part where the vet called and begged for us to pick him up because he was being too annoying.

Lastly, I want to acknowledge all the readers

who might pick up this book as you are dealing with your own worries. I see you! Your worries are real! But you aren't alone dealing with anxiety. There are a lot of people out there just like you—I am certainly one of them! I've found that the best thing to do was talk to someone like Mrs. Hines . . . or write letters to your dog . . . or find comfort in true friends who have your back no matter what. If all else fails, please reach out to me on Instagram at @saracshepard! I'd love to hear all about your worry lamps—and I'd love to hear what you think of Penny and her crew.

Penny's story continues in

A SCHOOL PLAY

Turn the page for a sneak peek!

PENNY DRAWS A SCHOOL PLAY

Dear Cosmo,

It's hard to believe it's winter. The time has gone so fast! I've barely had to write to you at all! But things are going great. And even though my mom became more and more pregnant—seems she really *is* having twins—we got used to the idea of having two babies in the family in a few months.

In other words, life was good! I couldn't complain!

Until this happened.

Unfortunately, those folded-paper fortune thingies NEVER LIE. The very next day, we got a new teacher. And she had some things to say about the fifth-grade play—which I'd been hoping to avoid, because I'm terrified to get onstage.

And what's worse? Nearly right after that happened, my mom said we were going on a "drive" after school. I figured she was tricking me into getting a flu shot, or maybe she was dragging me to another baby store to buy even more burp cloths and bottles. Who knew babies needed so much stuff?

She took us into this new neighborhood, drove up to this house, and got out and stood on the lawn. Then she said something surprising.

But . . . I liked our *current* house! I liked my neighborhood! I liked being a few streets away from Kristian! Although . . . he's mentioned something about doing a podcast about these noises he thinks he hears in his woods. He says it's Bigfoot!

Yet it seemed we didn't have a choice. Mom and Dad made up their minds—we were moving.

Am I ready for all these changes . . . AND to be expected to act in my huge school play? I'm not sure I can handle any of it!

Better not eat any more gum, Cosmo. Because I'm gonna need you by my side!

ABOUT THE AUTHOR

SARA SHEPARD is the author of the #1 *New York Times* bestselling series Pretty Little Liars, along with many other novels for young adults and adults. The Penny Draws series is her first one for younger readers. She lives in Pennsylvania with her husband, dogs, and sons Henry (who would have been named Penelope James had he been born a girl) and Kristian (who, like the character, loves all things roller coasters, especially riding them and talking about them).